The Almost All-White Rabbity Cat

The Almost
All-White
Rabbity Cat

Meindert DeJong

Illustrated by H. B. Vestal

The Macmillan Company
New York, New York

The Macmillan Company, 866 Third Avenue, New York, N.Y. 10022
Collier-Macmillan Canada Ltd., Toronto, Ontario

Library of Congress catalog card number: 72–178599

Printed in the United States of America

10 9 8 7 6 5 4 3 2 1

Entirely for Hugh and
for Marion McElwee

To be bored
is to be a block of wood
with no carving inside,
no river for drifting,
no fire for burning,
no nail.
Frederick ten Hoor

Contents

The Almost All-White Rabbity Cat

1

Two Goldfish in a Bowl

This day in the new apartment in the new city Barney got a cat that looked like a white rabbit. That was miraculous, because all his life back in his home village in the mountains Barney had had all-white rabbits for pets. Thirty white rabbits in thirty wire hutches in his grandfather's barn, row on row against the back wall.

The hutches ran as high as Barney could reach—only by stepping from a nail keg onto a pickle barrel, then standing on top of the pickle barrel he could feed and clean the rabbits. But always the hutches seemed to have to go higher, row on row, tier on tier, because rabbits get little rabbits, then little rabbits grow big and need hutches of their own to have their own little rabbits, and the only place left for more rabbits was up and up, row on row, tier on tier, rabbit hutch above rabbit hutch, white rabbit above white rabbit. But Grandpa had said, "Oh, there'll be more. There'll be more—until the hutches go right through the roof. If there's thirty white rabbits there'll be more!"

Grandpa had said that it was INEVITABLE.

Grandpa also had said that in a few years—oh, long before Barney could grow sideburns or need to shave—the whole barn, beginning right at the door, would be solid with rabbits. The barn would look like a jail with rows and rows of wire hutches, rising higher and higher with elbow-narrow aisles in between. Aisles only just wide enough for eternally cleaning and eternally feeding the everlastingly nibbling, eternally multiplying white rabbits clear up to the roof. "After that," Grandpa had solemnly told Barney, "after that you had better start practicing flying to reach the top rows on top of the roof. But that's what comes of thirty white rabbits."

It had sounded awesome. It had almost made Barney believe that maybe thirty white rabbits were about thirty too many—well, at least twenty-nine too many.

Now Barney sat in the little apartment looking at goldfish, but thinking about rabbits and grinning about Grandpa, but his grin went away when he also thought about what his grandfather had said. Grandpa had said there was a neat way out of the problem—eat the rabbits!

Barney couldn't have been more astounded if Grandpa had said he was going to eat *him*.

Barney had not been able to imagine eating pets. Not even one. Think of eating roast pet rabbit! With lettuce and cabbage and turnip tops, exactly all those things that the rabbit loved. It'd be as easy to eat Grandma!

Right then Barney had had to leave Grandpa and run —run all the awful roast rabbit thoughts out of himself. He had run all the way home to the other side of the mountain village. Home was behind the family grocery store. There'd been no one there, of course—Father and Mother had been up front tending the store, and he hadn't bothered them because he'd still had to run, so he'd run around the village the steep, upward way until he'd got back to Grandpa's yard. He'd not gone in the barn to Grandpa, he'd gone in the house to Grandma instead. The long hard run, the steep way, had made him hungry and he'd known there'd be fried fish for lunch, because the day before, Grandpa and he had gone cat-fish fishing in the river. Barney had been mouth-watering ready for fish, he loved eating fried fish. The fish hadn't been pets.

After the soul-satisfying meal of fish, he had gone right back to his rabbits. He lived for his pets, Grandpa always said, and it was a good thing the hutches were small, otherwise Barney would have crawled right in with his rabbits. Grandpa had said he thought it was right that Barney had been named after a barn, since except for school and some now-and-then fishing time, he practically lived in a barn. Barney hadn't minded at all—not when the barn held thirty white rabbits. White rabbits were wonderful.

Now all the wonderfulness of his rabbits was in the past, as was the mountain village, as was Grandpa, as was Grandma, as was fishing, as was everything. The white rabbits were Grandpa's now to pet and clean, to feed and to care for. Barney had had to leave them with Grandpa. His grandfather had looked most doubtful when Barney had made him a present of the rabbits, and even though Grandma had hugged him, Grandpa had sounded dubious when he'd said: "In a way, thirty rabbits are better than going fishing—at least, that is, on rainy days. On rainy days you can hardly go fishing, but there'll be thirty rabbits to take care of—if that makes a rainy day better."

But now Barney sat in a tiny apartment on the ground floor of a big apartment building in a strange city and all there was to do was to look at two goldfish in a bowl. He stared at the goldfish, but all he saw was a dark barn in a village high up on a mountain, and in the barn thirty white rabbits looking at him with their red eyes. It made Barney sigh so hard, the sigh stirred the surface of the water in the goldfish bowl. He sighed again and stirred the water more. It was all gone, everything he'd always loved, and now all he had was two dumb goldfish. He was bored. It was boring and dull—all the fish did was swim with their stupid round mouths open. All they could do was to make blubbery, slobbery sounds on the surface of their bit of still water.

At that dullest of all dull moments, the almost all-white cat came to him. Came to him in the tiny, silent apartment on the most impossible of rainy days when there was nothing but rain, and two goldfish. The white cat must have been in the building, because it had rained all morning and she was dry.

The first thing Barney knew of the all-white cat was a scratchy noise. Barney thought it was a mouse and he sat mouse-still on his stool. Because it was such a rain-gloomy day he had left all the lights on—even the one in the tiny entry hall. He could see it plainly as he leaned forward, and his eyes got big with surprise because it wasn't a mouse, it was a white paw, white as any rabbit's, that came poking under the hall door. But this paw was upside down! Now another paw, upside down too, slid under the door and over the green carpet. White paws!

The pads on the upturned paws were as pink as the pads of any white rabbit. But it was a cat—there were claws.

A cat! Oh, if he could only have a cat in here with him. Could he sneak to the door, jerk it open and grab the surprised cat before it could run? Aw, but a cat that could hear the slightest mouse sounds would hear him come, and run. Dang it, and he'd promised Mother up and down and sideways—she was so scared of this big town—that when he was alone he'd never leave the apartment, not as much as one step.

Barney glanced around for something to lure the cat through the door into the apartment, saw a small piece of paper under the telephone and grabbed it. He poked in his pocket for the piece of string that he kept just for knotting and unknotting. He crumpled the small sheet of paper and tied the string around one end so tight that the other end cupped and flared out like a skirt. If he danced the cupped paper along the crack under the door, then when the cat started to follow it, he'd ease the door open and lead the cat inside with the dancing, crackling paper. Then quick shut the door, and he'd have a cat.

Quietly, quietly Barney tiptoed to the entrance so as not to scare the cat away. Carefully, carefully he dropped to his knees and swished and rattled the paper just above the reaching white paws. But the paws curled up and claws seized the paper and ripped it and its whole string away under the door. Down on his knees Barney could hear the paper tearing to shreds under the cat's nails. His scheme of luring the cat was over before it had begun.

Now there wasn't a sound outside the door. The cat must have gone away. Disappointed, Barney got up from the floor, but when he looked down the white paws came sliding out over the carpet again. They pulled back under the door. In the stillness there came the tiniest slight click of the lock, and the door sprang open. Barney stood looking down at a white cat. The cat looked up at Barney. But it didn't run. It rolled over, got on its feet and all tail-up friendly it marched itself past the astounded Barney straight into the living room to the goldfish bowl.

Speechless, Barney looked not at the cat but at the wide-open door and at the tiny nail-torn and chewed shreds of paper strewn over the hall carpet. Barney stood, still not believing his eyes—not believing the open door!

Then he turned. The cat had jumped onto the table with the goldfish bowl. He slammed the door shut and ran to the living room to grab the cat. He sank down with her on the stool, looked from the door to the cat and looked again, for in his arms the cat felt as woolly white as any white rabbit. Why, she was such a rabbity cat, it was as if she had come through a locked door to take the place of his thirty white rabbits. It was unbelievable. He

looked at the cat closely. She wasn't all white like his rabbits—at least her tail wasn't, and for some reason that made him feel a little better. Her tail was ringed the way a raccoon's tail is ringed, and going from the root of her tail out over her back there were three round spots the same smudgy gray as the rings on her tail, each spot about as big and as round as a silver dollar. But that made it all the more amazing that the cat could look so all-white and so rabbity.

In his puzzlement over the cat's managing to look so all-white and so rabbity, Barney almost forgot being surprised over the cat's opening a locked door and coming in. But no matter how she had come in, if she wanted to stay here he wanted her—more even than all his thirty white rabbits.

The cat did not look up at Barney, but sat in his lap looking only at the two goldfish. Then, surprisingly, she twisted her face up at him and with a rosy-pink tongue showing between her pale-pink lips she begged Barney for the goldfish.

"You can't have two goldfish," Barney told her as if he'd always known her. "You can't even have one. No, you can't, Rosita. Hey, that's what I'm going to call you —Rosita! It sort of means pink, I think. If you stay, that's what I'll call you, Rosita."

It was such a right name it seemed to make the cat his,

and he gave her a quick, hard squeeze. Rosita squeaked a little but she wasn't alarmed. She dipped her pink nose down in the crook of his arm and began to purr for him—a nice, soft, delicate little motor run of a purr.

To Barney her purr was like singing. Rosita was singing him a white-cat song without words and without any ending. The purr that had just begun of itself didn't have to stop for a breath, didn't have to pause for a swallow—it just sang itself on.

Rabbits couldn't purr. It was a treacherous thought. Well, Rosita couldn't wriggle her nose or make her chin go nibble-nibble when she ate, so they were even. Still, rabbits *couldn't* purr.

As if the cat knew Barney was thinking of his rabbits, she did a nice, soft, sleepy thing. Right in her purring she pulled one paw out of Barney's arm and reached up and held it to the middle of his cheek. She kept it there, softly pressed to the hollow of Barney's cheek, all her claws sheathed and pulled safely down inside the pink pads of her paws.

Then Barney had to talk to her. She was the first thing he'd talked to since early in the long rainy morning when Father and Mother had left for work. Barney wanted to talk, talk, and talk—but how did you talk to a cat? Maybe the way a cat talked?

Barney made little mutters, trying to spin deep down

in his throat a sort of rumble that would sound like a purr. At his first rumble the white cat sat up, alarmed. Barney hastily softened his rumble. Rosita cocked her white head to listen and to consider.

Then—as if she approved—she began purring in a new voice herself, as if she were saying: "Such as it is, such as it is, Barney, it's a very good try, and it will pass, but only just pass. Such as it is—I don't mind it too much—such as it is."

She looked at Barney steadily, then as if to make it right, she lifted her little white face and her pink mouth and kissed him.

Surprised, Barney jerked around and looked back of him to see if anyone had seen this wondrous thing of a cat kissing him. Of course, no one had. There was no one to see, no one but the goldfish. And no one could see through the window. Outside there was nothing but rain and the darkness of rain. He was alone.

It made Barney feel silly, the way he had jerked around. And Rosita did not kiss him again, did not reach up her white paw to touch his cheek. Instead she turned away from him, and from his knee rested the outstretched paw against the rounding of the goldfish bowl. The two goldfish stared at the white paw.

But Barney looked at it in amazement, thinking what strange things this white cat had done. In just these few minutes, all kinds of tricks! Rabbits didn't have tricks like that—rabbits didn't have any tricks. But Rosita, who was as soft and woolly white as a rabbit, was smart as anything. Oh, she was smart—and loving! Rabbits weren't smart, and rabbits weren't loving at all—not to people.

Now from jerking around to see if anybody had seen a cat kissing him, Barney was eager to tell somebody about Rosita. Of course, there wasn't anybody to tell anything to, and Barney had to tell himself that there wouldn't have been anybody to tell it to back in the village either. Kissing a cat—would that have made him sound like a darn fool! How they'd have kidded him in the village!

Barney looked down at the white cat stretched out asleep in his lap, her one paw touching the goldfish bowl. No, back home he couldn't have told any other kid either—oh, maybe just some girl. Tell some girl close by, that you knew real well, all about Rosita's loving tricks. A girl much younger and littler. That way, if you were alone with a girl like that—no other kids standing around—maybe you could even show her Rosita kissing you!

Barney wistfully looked out the window. There was no one there either, of course. Beyond the window there was nothing but the thick, driven curtains of rain in a wide, busy street. There was only the watery swish sound of passing cars. There was no one and nobody, and he knew no one in this whole town. There wasn't even anybody in the apartment building that he knew. He'd bet there wasn't one other kid his age in the whole building. There was nobody.

Why, but that was exactly right! Since there was nobody, nobody could know the white cat was with him here in the apartment. Nobody knew.

Barney looked down at the sleeping cat in triumph. Here he'd been feeling bad that there was nobody, and it had turned out that that was the best thing, if he wanted to keep Rosita. Nobody knew, nobody could know. As if to make the cat wholly his own, Barney softly stroked her as she lay sleeping. And the goldfish stared out of the goldfish bowl.

2

Hot Dogs in a Cat

It was noon. There was no clock in the room, but Barney knew it was noon by the clock in his stomach—he was hungry. He'd had to be still because of the sleeping cat in his lap, but now he couldn't sit still from hunger. The white cat must have a clock inside her, too. She stirred and immediately jumped down from Barney's lap. She stopped where she'd landed and stood looking up with green-flecked, greedy eyes at the goldfish. She let out such a hoarse, raw miaou Barney jumped. He'd expected a tiny, meek miaou from such a small mouth, but Rosita sounded as if she had a bad cold. No, Barney decided, listening, it sounded more as if Rosita were saying a string of cat curses so fast you couldn't quite catch the words.

"Whatever you're saying—and you shouldn't be saying it that way—you can't have the goldfish," Barney told her.

She didn't want them. To show Barney what she wanted, Rosita galloped tail up to the kitchen. She actually galloped, at least she made small galloping noises on the kitchen linoleum. She ran to the refrigerator as if she knew all about what refrigerators were for.

"How's for hot dogs for lunch?" Barney asked the cat. "But it'll be without buns—my mother forgot them last night. How many hot dogs can a cat eat? Hey, that's something—hot dogs in a cat."

Then Barney considered. He did not know how much a cat could eat, but there'd be no buns and since it was Mother who had forgotten them, he had no compunction about dropping the whole package of hot dogs into the water he was heating. If Rosita and he needed them, they'd eat them all.

They started to eat together. But it was more together than Barney had counted on. Rosita looked dainty and white but she had no table manners. When Barney dipped all the hot dogs out of the boiling water onto one plate— one plate was less dishes to wash—Rosita jumped right onto the table to eat from his plate with him. She actually started to drag one hot dog over the edge of the plate. Barney had to slap her down—she'd burn her mouth. But Rosita was so hungry she jumped right back onto the table. Then luckily Barney remembered that not only had the former tenants of this apartment left the goldfish behind—they'd also left a highchair in one of the closets. Hey, was that a thought! He grabbed Rosita under one arm, ran to the closet and dragged the high-chair to the kitchen.

It proved exactly right for Rosita and she seemed to know about highchairs. She jumped into it before Barney had quite pushed it up to the table. She sat properly in the chair, put her two front feet on the edge of the metal baby tray before her, opened her mouth and demanded food in her raw, hoarse, cursing, food voice. Hey, she could curse even better than Grandpa!

Barney explained to Rosita that she had to wait until the hot dogs cooled, that she'd burn her mouth. It sounded silly to be talking about her little pink mouth and she cursing, but it was hard to know how to talk to a cat.

Barney spread the hot dogs apart so they would cool as fast as possible. He shoved them out of reach to the middle of the table and went to fetch a knife to cut up a wiener for Rosita. But she had no patience with it, she was that hungry—it surely must mean that though she lived in the building she belonged to no one, and was starved. Barney plunked down a whole hot dog in the baby tray. Hastily he remembered to test it for heat on

the back of his hand—the way mothers did for babies. Rosita did not recognize a whole hot dog as food, her white paw shot out, and she stirred it all round her tray, she leaned out and sniffed at it, but she didn't bite into it. At least stirring it around on cold metal cooled the hot dog some more, but Rosita played with it as if it were a limp, boiled mouse.

Barney cut it up for her, but standing over the tray with the peppery smell of the hot dog steaming up into his nostrils made him hungry all over. Hungry as he was Barney still divided it honestly—a thin slice of hot dog for Rosita, and a long chunk of hot dog for him, each one in turn. His pieces were bigger, three times bigger, but then he was at least five or six times bigger than the cat.

In no time, eating together like that, they'd eaten the white plate empty. Barney stared at it forlornly, he was still hungry. My, hot dogs ate fast with no buns and no chili and no sauce and mustard. If you ate them sort of naked like that they were soon gone, and he and Rosita had just started. Barney looked around the bare neatness of the kitchen, but he couldn't think of anything else for their lunch except milk. He poured milk for Rosita right into her highchair tray, and he himself drank from the bottle. No dishes that way, and glasses all milk-cloudy were a big pain to wash. One paper towel was enough to wipe the wetness from the white plate, then Barney used it to scrub out Rosita's tray, and like that they were done, with no dishes to wash. Barney turned the pan in which he'd heated the hot dogs upside down in the sink. Pans were for Mother. He put what was left of the milk in the refrigerator—then all was done. Why, he hadn't even sat down to eat, he'd just stood over the highchair and waited on Rosita! Well, that wasn't so bad because now all there was left to do was to sit down all the rest of the whole day until Mother and Dad got home. And always it rained—rained and rained—as if it mattered, he couldn't go out anyway.

Barney looked up at the kitchen clock. And only now it was exactly twelve o'clock noon. Hey, both his and Rosita's stomachs must have been way early!

"It's noon," Barney solemnly told Rosita and pulled at his lip trying to think what to do next. He looked wistfully at the refrigerator—if there were more hot dogs they could do it again. Gosh, he was still hungry. That's what came from bolting your food. But Mother always said that if you bolted your food and ate things too fast, they would sort of after-feed themselves inside you, if you just waited. Well, that sure was the only thing they could do—sit in the living room and look at the goldfish and see if the hot dogs would after-feed. It sounded dull, long and boring.

From the kitchen Barney looked at the goldfish bowl but beyond it on the table saw the telephone, and that reminded him. Very brightly, and as if it were a great thing, he told the silent cat, "It's noon. Soon after that, Mother calls from where she works to check on me. She's worried that I'm here alone all day, but she won't let me go out! She's scared of the traffic in this busy town. Anyway, it's raining. But wait until she calls today! Wait till I tell her I've got a cat with me in the apartment!"

Rosita yawned and began to wash her face after her big meal. She acted as if she was too full. Barney resented that. Why, come to think of it he must be easily ten, twelve times bigger than she, so she'd had three times too much hot dog and he hadn't had enough. But what could you do about it now? He'd better get his mind off hot dogs.

"Mother is never going to believe it," Barney tried to say brightly. "She isn't going to believe I've got you in here." He chortled at the surprise it was going to be to Mother on the other end of the phone. Then out of his chortling he stared at the white cat. "Of course, Mother won't believe it," he said slowly. "She can't believe it, the door was locked. You couldn't get in unless you had a key. How is she going to believe you came in through a locked door?"

Barney talked loud and excited right into Rosita's face.

For a moment she went on washing then she looked up at Barney annoyed, jumped down from her highchair

and ran to the entry hall. Without hesitating a moment
she threw herself down on the floor, pushed her paws
under the locked door and lifted until there was a click.
At that tiny click the door unlocked and sprang open.
Rosita had to jump up fast to keep the door from swing-
ing against her. She jumped back, the door swung wide
and Rosita, ring tail proudly straight up, marched
through the open doorway into the hall.

The moment she was in the hall she looked back, saw
Barney coming and streaked white-flat down the long
dim hall. In one flying leap out of the entry Barney took
after her, but already the white cat was racing around
the corner into a connecting hall and then she was gone.

From the hard thud of Barney's leap, the apartment
door swung shut and the lock clicked. Then inside the
apartment the telephone began shrilling. It rang and
rang, demanding him to come, and Barney rattled and
tugged at the knob, shook the door, kicked the door, but
it stayed locked. Mother was calling to check on him,
but he was locked out and if he didn't answer she'd worry
herself sick. He wasn't supposed to be out of the apartment.

The telephone stopped, but Barney waited. Then at
last he started a few steps away from the door to see if
Rosita could be seen anywhere.

The telephone began again. This time it did not quit,

it kept ringing on and on, shrill and angry. Barney threw himself against the door, it didn't yield. Then he did what he had seen the white cat do—dropped to the floor, rolled over, pushed his fingertips under the door and lifted. In between the rings of the telephone there was a tiny click. To Barney it sounded like a gunshot. Fingertips still under the door, he butted against it with the top of his head. And, as it had happened with Rosita, the door sprang open, slid over his outstretched fingers and thudded against the wall. Barney ran for the phone. As he reached out for it, the telephone stopped, but he snatched the receiver and yelled, "Mom! Mom, I'm here. Mom!"

There was no answer. He slammed the receiver down and grabbed for the slip of paper kept under the telephone—the paper on which Mother had written her telephone number and Dad's number. His heart sank as he remembered he'd used the paper to play with the cat under the door, and that now it was shredded to confetti. He started for the door, but there was no use, there wasn't enough left to fit together and read the numbers. In his dismay all he could think of was that Dad's number was different from Mother's even though they worked for the same company. He sank down on the stool and tried to remember. No, he couldn't. It was all so new. So much had happened in this first week of the new town, the new apartment. There'd been so much talk about the new job—it was all confused in his mind. All Barney could remember was that Dad was learning how to become the manager of a big supermarket, and Mother was learning to be his bookkeeper and buyer, so they could run a store for a grocery chain in this city or in some other big place. But there had been so much talk. Then Rosita had come, and now even Rosita was gone.

He must find her, that's what he must do. He could unlock the door from the outside now. He could get back in any time. He could go and look on all the seven floors of the building, and then simply go back into the apartment without anyone having to know at all.

He ran to the door, pulled it open and just let it fall shut and lock itself behind him. He raced down the hall to find Rosita.

3

Knock on Every Door

It had been easy to decide that he had to find Rosita, but once Barney had run down all the four halls he didn't know what to do next. There had been no white cat down any hall. All there had been was silent dimness except for the dot islands of light made by the bare bulbs in the ceilings. That was all, dots of light and dimness and quiet, and no signs of life anywhere.

Barney was back where he'd started, before the closed door of his own apartment. It was no different from all the other doors except for its number. And behind his closed door there was silence too—no telephone rang. No telephone rang anywhere, no cat moved, no voices of people sounded. It was so still that Barney could hear the rain drearily falling outside. That's all there was—rain.

Somehow Barney couldn't go in. He started off again. He wanted to run and run over the soft carpeted halls so that it pounded out behind him, so that doors would open, and people would look, and somebody would help him.

But now he had to think what was to be done next. Yelling and running wouldn't do it, thinking it out maybe would. He stared along the row of white doors—white doors, white light, but no white cat.

A scared thought flashed into Barney's mind. What if Rosita had gone outside? He had to find out if she could open the outside door. That was one thing he could do.

At the big door he tried with two fingers of one hand; he couldn't do it. He tried pushing it with what he considered would be the strength of a cat. He couldn't do it. Then he thought that really wasn't fair—he was pushing against the middle of the door. Rosita would have to push against the bottom. He lay down, he pushed with his fingers, pushed with one flat hand, pushed with two flat hands, and then the door opened.

When Barney looked up, an old lady coming in had opened the door. She'd *pulled* it open. Barney felt foolish, lying there on the floor in a public doorway. He put his face in his hands and made little murmur sounds as if he were counting out to himself for hide-and-seek. But he kept one eye open, saw the old lady shake her head, and then just take a big, high step over him. From her big step she looked back at Barney and said, "Hide-and-seek, hunh? Wish I could play."

Then she was gone, and down the hall a door slammed before Barney could call after her: "I'll play with you!" And he'd never thought to ask did she know Rosita. But he mustn't say *Rosita*, that was only his name for her. What should he say? Oh, maybe, had she ever seen a white rabbity cat with a sort of raccoon tail? No, he'd better not say rabbity, these were city people, city people didn't keep rabbits; they had no barns. And rabbits were rather smelly—all right for barns but not for apartments. Hardly!

Grinning about that, Barney brightened. Now he knew what to do. The old lady who'd just stepped over him without any fuss had given him an idea. He'd knock on her door and then on every door and ask about Rosita. If they knew her they might know in which apartment she lived. If they didn't know her he'd go on every floor until he found her. He had to have her. Why in the little time he'd had her she, all by herself, had almost taken the place of his thirty white rabbits.

In high hopes Barney boldly marched from the entrance to where he thought he'd heard the high-stepping old lady slam her door. But it was just a guess—Barney's hopes started dropping. Standing there with his knocking fist raised made him doubtful. It seemed impossible to knock. What if it wasn't the nice old lady? What would he say? What if a big man opened the door? What would he say to strangers? Could he say: "Lady,"—if it was a lady—"have you seen an almost white cat, except she's got a ring tail?" That didn't make sense. City people didn't know about raccoons, raccoons didn't clamber around in apartment buildings. They'd maybe know about Easter rabbits—but not raccoons.

He tried again. "She's sort of a rabbity white cat," he explained to an imaginary woman. "Do you know of a cat like that?" Oh, it sounded nuts! "White rabbity!" The woman would slam the door and then behind the locked door she'd run to the phone and call the police: "Police, police! There's a crazy kid here asking about rabbity cats that have raccoon tails. Bring your patrol wagon and a stretcher and handcuffs, and bring a strait jacket too—bring everything!"

In the silent hall Barney tried to chuckle and chortle at his own joke, but it came out more like a snorkle than a chortle—a snorkle under water. He dropped his hand and wished that the door had a bell button. Knocking on a stranger's door and making him come out to you made you feel as if you were acting like a policeman. Doorbells were much easier.

Since the door had no bell it gave Barney the excuse to ease away and drift down the hall to look for a door with a bell, knowing very well it was just an excuse for not knocking on *any door*. But he ought to knock on every door. Hey, there was a door with a doorbell! The door was different, it wasn't white, it was gray, and it was metal. Maybe it was where the janitor lived and he would know about everybody in the whole building and if a white-rabbity-ring-tailed cat belonged to anybody in this building. Maybe Rosita was the janitor's cat. . . .

It *was* ten times easier to push the bell than to raise a fist to a tight-closed door. He quickly touched the bell, then turned and stood looking in triumph at all the doors that had needed knocking on. This was done with one little push. Funny, he thought, if there had been one other kid—just one—there'd have been nothing to it to knock on any door. They'd just have done it, because with two of you you wouldn't stand thinking about it. But there was no use thinking—there were no kids here that he knew about. There were only young people before they had kids or people so old that if they had children they must be grandchildren—at least that's all he'd ever seen from his window.

Behind Barney there came a slow, tired sighing. He

whirled around and there before his eyes the gray, sighing door slid open. It was an elevator! Startled, Barney stepped on it for no reason except that the door had opened for him. The moment he had done so the door slid shut. There was a whole battery of white buttons before Barney's face, one for each of the seven floors and one marked B. That must mean basement. He'd never been on a self-help elevator before. Now which button to push? The one for the basement? But what would be down there but mice? Barney grinned as he imagined Rosita saying to him in her raw, cursing voice, "Come on, Barney, get with it. Let's go to the basement."

Imagining Rosita saying that seemed so real, it made him hopeful of finding her. He decided to stop the elevator on all seven floors and run around all the four halls on each floor. He'd start up, and if by the time he reached the seventh floor he still had not found Rosita, he'd shoot straight down to the basement.

It was good to run again. So good that when Barney got out at the third floor he made a flying leap to the hall, then he raced around it to see if he could beat the elevator's slow, sighing door. He lost. But fast as he'd run he'd looked everywhere and he knew that Rosita wasn't on this floor. Unless, of course, she was inside one of the apartments.

He lost to the elevator on every floor, he expected to, but he improved on his game, and on the sixth floor he actually saw the door begin sliding shut. With a loud, rebel yell he made a flying leap into the elevator. It caught his heel and flung him to the floor—shutting off his yell and leaving it behind in the hall.

If it had been good to run as hard as he could six times, to yell out in the stillness had been even better. When he burst from the elevator at the seventh and last floor, he ran hardest of all down all the four halls and let his wild yells stream out behind him. The yells made doors open, voices sounded, scared questions flew in the air, a woman called out, "Call the police!" Barney looked back but saw no one. But for all of his hard running he missed the elevator door. Behind him people had come out in the hall and were asking loud questions. One woman shouted right at Barney, and a man's voice threatened him from another direction. Rattled and scared, Barney still remembered that on every floor just beyond the elevator he had seen white doors marked STAIRWAY.

He scooted, head ducked out, as if to pull his body around the corner.

"What's that kid doing here?" the big man thundered. "He's got no business—no kids allowed here." His words chased Barney around the corner to the stairway door.

Barney jerked it open and was three steps up, before

he remembered to reach down and pull the top of the door shut behind him. He stood panting and listening. He couldn't go back—not with all the people his yelling had brought to the halls. What had made him do it? It was the silent carpet, the silent halls, the tight-closed doors and Rosita nowhere. But it didn't help now to know why. Noiselessly Barney turned to see what was ahead of him.

Above, the dark stairway led to a closed trap door. There on the top step, white in the darkness, crouched Rosita! From her ring tail a cobweb waved like a filmy flag. It made Barney feel much better—it was like the cobwebs in Grandpa's barn, and it showed that the stairway was seldom used. But he couldn't go back with Rosita in his arms—not with all the people in the halls—and if anybody came here they were caught under the trap door. They'd have to go up. It was what Rosita seemed to want too, the way she scrubbed her head against the underside of the cobwebby door. She pleaded for it in a tiny kitten voice Barney had not heard from her before. She waited for him. This must be one door she could not open.

Barney pushed up. The trap door was hardly open a crack before Rosita squirmed through. Barney did not dare to be noisy. He had to ease the door straight up, then slowly let it swing back and down on the roof. Now

rain fell on his upturned face. He and Rosita were on the high roof in the rain.

Rain pelted in Barney's eyes, rain washed down his upturned face as he stood unsure of the high roof. He was a little bit scared. He knew he wasn't doing right. Mother had never said in so many words about not getting on the roof but that was because Mother had never thought of the roof seven stories up—anyhow, he wasn't supposed to go out of the apartment at all. But now Rosita was gone from sight, she couldn't be seen anywhere. He had to go out on the roof to get her. Oh, there she was, she'd crawled under the tipped-back trap door to get out of the rain. Barney had to get down on his knees in a deep puddle to reach her at all. He made a grab but she slipped from under his hand, and all he caught was the bedraggled soaked cobweb that had wrapped itself around her tail.

In spite of the rain Rosita scooted out from under the far end of the door and across the roof. Then Barney saw there were birds sheltering under a beach umbrella that must have been set up for them, for underneath it lay scattered seed. There was a whirr of wings as the flattened cat streaked under the red-striped umbrella, white paws slashing and flashing. The birds got away, and Rosita came down from her upward leap with only one black tail feather in her outstretched paws. She snuffed at the feather and dropped it, then sniffed disconsolately among the damp birdseed, her tail lashing her sides as if she were punishing herself for being so clumsy.

Barney could almost feel sorry for her, so wet for nothing. It must be hard for a white cat to catch things—she was so showy. But he worried about the seed. It must be that in spite of the cobwebs somebody came up here every day to feed the birds. It must be that whoever fed the birds left the trap door wide open, except when it rained, and Rosita had found out about it and came here for the birds. They had to get out of here. Here they were trapped. Barney rubbed a wet hand over his wet face. "Let's go," he said to Rosita and stooped under the fancy umbrella, but Rosita ran straight for the little low wall that ran around the outer edge of the roof. Barney raced after her. There were guttering, deep puddles in all the hollows of the flat roof and across the whole roof, where it was level, rain water raced shiny black over the tar. Rosita skirted the deeper puddles and ran on in a high-legged run, almost as if she were a woman holding her skirts high against the splashing. Then, down on the low wall, almost down in the mouth of the white cat, a bedraggled wet sparrow stupidly landed. Without a useless move, and without looking, Rosita sailed to the wall, paws out, claws out and ready. On the outer edge the landing sparrow fluttered backward and fell from Barney's view behind the low wall. Rosita reached down with both paws for the sparrow, some way holding herself on the wall by her set, spread hind legs. She tried to grab the sparrow out of the air. She was seven stories up!

Behind her Barney didn't dare move—didn't dare call out to Rosita. In slow motion he advanced until his knees touched the wall, then stooped, hands ready to grab Rosita's hind legs—he mustn't miss, he couldn't make a sound.

In that dreadful slow motion Barney was looking seven stories down a brick canyon to the faraway ground between two buildings. He saw Rosita studying a cat down in the areaway between the buildings. Down there was a caterwauling tomcat, sniffing his way from basement window to basement window. In the windows, sheltered from rain, he sniffed over the glass as he wailed. The rain suddenly stopped and Rosita looked up at Barney's scared face and pulled herself up, then sat on the edge of the wall and began wash-drying herself. She did not answer the tomcat, she disdainfully washed her white whiskers.

Above her, Barney let out his breath. There sat the cat—washing. He snatched her up in his arms, hugged her against his thumping chest and didn't stop with her until he was in the middle of the roof. There he had to stop, he was shaking so. There had been nothing below them but hard cement—seven stories down! Hard cement and one mangy tomcat. Barney backed into the beach umbrella. Its long pole bent so hard it squeaked. Rosita, scared, twisted and pulled out of Barney's clutch. She leaped to the umbrella. The squeak of its pole gave Barney an idea. He ducked under the umbrella and began to chirp like a sparrow. Rosita swarmed over the rounding of the umbrella and jumped down onto his neck. He grabbed her and hauled her down.

He had been so scared that only now he noticed that the rain had stopped. All around them on the high roof the rain-washed city rose high and beautiful. Suddenly the sun blinked from out of a hole in the clouds, and a moment's rainbow came into the sky and faded as it came. Then the clouds scudded away from over the city and a blue sky came to stand first above the buildings and then over the green hills.

Under the blue, far beyond the high, stiff buildings, silver flashed—long silver. Long, because it was the river, and now with the dark rain gone boats could be seen easing along it. And over the river's bridges bug-sized cars crawled. A bridge rose in the air for one of the boats and looked from this distance as if it rose by its own magic. Out in the country beyond the river's silver the blue of the sky leaned on the hills.

"The river," Barney whispered. "Look, Rosita, my river. We followed it all the way from our village up in the mountains. It's my river—it's wild and white and it foams out there in the mountains where Grandpa and I go fishing."

He said no more. He ran for the stairway. "We've got to run because it's going to rain again," he told the cat. But he ran to get away from the river. His river.

To let the trap door down he had to let Rosita down. He gave her a hard shove to send her down the stairs. He was never going to come here again!

At the bottom of the stairs he picked up Rosita. He eased the door open a crack, but there was no one in the hall. Still, Barney did not dare take the elevator down. They'd be as trapped in the elevator, if someone got on, as they'd been on the roof. Door after door, stairway after stairway, Barney stole all the way back to the ground floor with Rosita. Then he raced with her along the silent carpet to his own door. He threw himself down on the floor with Rosita. She squeezed away from him, but she did not run. She watched as he pushed his fingertips under the door to unlock it. Then she walked the length of him, lay down beside him and pushed her paws under the door, too. She purred as she did it—he felt it against his cheek. She must be proud that he had learned to open the door. She wanted to open it with him.

4

River of Home

Together Barney and Rosita pushed up on the door. Nothing happened. They tried again, again nothing happened. Then without a sound the door slid from over their paws and fingertips.

Two eyes peered out, then the door was pulled open. It was Mother. Flat on his back Barney looked up. Mother stared down at him. "Mother, look at my cat," he stammered.

"What are you doing down there?" Mother's voice shook. "Get up off that floor!"

With a hopeful grin Barney turned to Rosita. Rosita was gone! Without a word Barney jumped up and raced

after the cat. She was not in the hall, not around the corner, not anywhere. Barney ran back to his own door. But
Mother was not there, she was running around the corner after him. He tore after her, his thoughts racing
faster than he. When he came to the stairway that led to
the second floor he hesitated. Should he catch up with
Mother or try the second floor for Rosita before she got
back to the roof? The roof! He couldn't let Mother know
about the roof. He'd go to her first and maybe together
they'd find Rosita before she got all the way up to the
roof.

Mother was now running down the back hall. He
grabbed her hand as he caught up to her. "Come on,"
he urged. "Hurry, we've got to find Rosita." He pulled
at her hand.

But Mother wouldn't pull—she wouldn't come. "Who
is Rosita?" she demanded.

"Rosita is the white cat you saw. I've got to find her,"
Barney puffed. "Hurry!"

Mother looked at Barney's worried face and began to
run with him. But after they'd run up the first stairway
she couldn't run anymore. She dropped down on the
dirty steps and whispered, "Barney." Her chest heaved.
When she got her breath she said firmly, "Never mind
the cat. I want to talk to you."

Barney pulled the stair door shut so no one would see

Mother sitting there like a naughty girl in a closet. Then he sat down on the edge of the step beside her. He was worried, Mother was so still, and it seemed as if she hadn't heard a word he had said about Rosita.

"Rosita's the white cat . . ." he began to explain.

But Mother broke in, "I ran all the way here from work—I couldn't find a taxi—then all the way up these stairs. I can't—I can't run anymore."

Maybe it was a good thing. It would give him time to think. Mother was so upset and scared . . . if she found out he'd been up on the roof. He shoved close, sometimes that helped, sitting close. If Rosita *had* gone up to the roof and the trap door was still closed, all she could do was sit there waiting for him. She'd have to wait until Mother, tired as she was, went back to work or back to the apartment. Then he could run up and get Rosita.

All at once Mother said, "Now with that cat and the way you feel about her, you'll go anywhere to find her, won't you? Even up on that dangerous roof—even in those busy streets . . ." Her voice shook. "But I can't go back to work knowing that! Barney, I want to go home."

Now he was scared. "You are home," he told her. "Mom, you are home!" Maybe she'd been so scared and worried about him, she'd gone crazy!

"I don't mean this," Mother said impatiently. "I mean home, really home. Back where we lived, where Grandpa and Grandma are."

Barney couldn't believe what Mother had just said, and he couldn't believe what was happening to him. He didn't want to go home, at least he didn't want to go without Rosita.

He heard himself saying right out to Mother, "If we go, we've first got to find Rosita. I won't go without her."

It was hardly the way to talk to his mother, so Barney spelled it out word by word. "If Rosita is nobody's, just an alley cat, we can take her home with us in the car. You'll like her, Mother, she's smart." Then as a clincher he added, "And Grandpa would like her around his barn to catch all the rats and mice that come for the rabbit feed. Mom, wouldn't it be wonderful if I could take my white rabbity cat back to all my white rabbits?"

"A cat like a rabbit?" Mother said in an unbelieving voice. She shook her head. "Oh, Barney, I don't really want to go back, I suppose. I want to stay so your father can become the manager of a big store, because that's what he wants. But if that's what he wants I'm afraid it'll have to be without me, because I'm going to stay here with you. It's been so awful this last week. You here and me working. Not knowing anybody in this whole city, everything strange and everybody a stranger."

The words poured out of Mother. "Barney," she interrupted herself, "where is this strange cat that looks like a rabbit, and that opens doors?"

Then Barney had to tell her what he didn't believe himself. "If Rosita can open our door," he explained, "then maybe she can open any other door in the building. Maybe she just ran into some other apartment when all of a sudden you opened our door and scared her away."

Mother was studying him. "Yes, and if I should go back to the office, you'd go through this whole building opening apartment doors to find her. If she can unlock doors, so can you. Barney, you mustn't! You mustn't even think of it. It would be dangerous—you don't know what might happen. And it would be like burglary, entering and stealing, even if you think she's your cat, it would be stealing. She isn't yours, just because she looks like your rabbits to you. You can't go into people's apartments. Did you have that in mind?"

"I never even thought of it. You did!" Barney said indignantly. He was hurt, but at the same time a bit disgusted that *he* hadn't thought of it. He didn't know what to say.

"Well, now that I've planted it in your mind you know it," Mother said. "And the moment I'm out of the way you'll do it."

"I won't either," Barney said weakly.

Mother didn't listen. "Now I certainly can't go back to that office," she decided. "I can't, whatever happens to the job. I imagine I'll be fired." She stood up and said as if to someone up the narrow stairs, "No, my mind is made up. I'll not go back this afternoon or any other afternoon. I'm needed here." She whipped around to Barney. "When you need something, you need it. And you seem to need that cat. Let's go find him—we'll knock on every door if we have to."

"It's her, not him," Barney told her. The way Mother changed in just moments! Her eyes were almost a little bit too wild for a mother.

Mother grabbed his shoulder, shoved him through the door and back into the hall. "Let's go and find that cat. I want to meet people, and joke and laugh. If we find your Rosita I'll talk her owner out of her, I'll buy her right there at the door."

Barney stood looking at her.

"Come on, come on, we'll hunt Rosita and meet people. If they won't come to their doors, we'll do like your cat, we'll push them open so they'll have to come to close them."

"Mother! After what you said about me opening doors!"

Mother tossed her head and laughed. "Oh, Barney, I was just talking. If I opened doors they'd throw me in jail. I want to be free—that wouldn't be free."

Barney thought of the roof, and Rosita most likely

waiting for him under the trap door. He had to get up there! Before Mother could knock on the first door he told her about the elevator that you worked yourself, all the way to the top floor. Maybe that would give him a chance to run up to Rosita. It worked. Mother was being so girl-gay she wanted to try the elevator at once. But when they got to the seventh floor, she wanted to take it right down again. Up and down they went—all the way up, all the way down. There wasn't a chance to get out of the elevator. Mother was like a kid with the panel of buttons. She was playing elevator operator.

It was silly.

When once more they got down to the ground floor, Mother actually got off the elevator and looked up and down the hall to see if there was anybody she could take up. So she *was* playing elevator operator!

"Mother, stop it!" Barney was desperate.

Mother looked at him, startled. "Tell me, is everything always like this in this building? You'd think it was a morgue. Don't you ever see anyone? Isn't anyone alive?"

"I don't know. I've been inside that apartment all week," Barney said.

"It must have been awful." Mother looked at him. "Barney, am I acting too wild?"

Barney nodded.

"Well, but don't you see, I've never had a week like this before. There's been nothing but work, and at night, meetings—like school—to learn the new business. And there are going to be two more weeks of it! If I had known of all those meetings at night after working all day, I'd have left you with Grandpa and Grandma. Sure, I worked in our little store at home, but that was different. It wasn't every minute of every day. Anyhow, I knew you were at school or at Grandpa's. Not inside a tiny apartment all alone! But now it's over, and never again. Come on, let's have fun."

Up they went again.

By the time Mother stopped the elevator on the seventh floor Barney was desperate enough to tell her about the roof. He didn't mention the little low wall and the mangy old tomcat all those naked miles down.

Mother was sorry at once. "Why didn't you tell me? Here I've been acting goofy and you worrying about your cat. Why didn't you say so? You shouldn't have gone up there, but since you did, I want to go up too. I want to do everything with you from now on."

"Everything?" Barney questioned in a small voice.

He wouldn't like that at all. He thought of the swimming hole where he and the other boys went skinny-dipping all summer. How they'd scream and run if Mother came with him. His grin ran all over his face.

"I thought you were so worried. What are you grinning about?" Mother asked suspiciously.

Barney changed the subject. "Mom, you can see our river from the roof."

Rosita wasn't crouched under the trap door. She wasn't waiting. Still, Mother wanted to go on the roof because of what he'd said about the river. The moment she stepped out she saw the whole blue of sunshiny sky over the green of the hills beyond the town—and then she saw the river. She stared and stared. Then she scuttled back to the stairway well without seeming to have noticed the low wall. She ran down the stairs as a sob broke from her throat. "I don't want to see it again," she called up to Barney. "I don't want to see it until we can go home along it. Oh, Barney, I do want to go home—this isn't home. Home is where the river is, where it comes from."

Barney could not say a thing.

"Come on," Mother said, "let's go down to our apartment, because I think I'm going to cry. But after I've sat still a little while, I promise you we'll go to every floor and knock on every door to find your Rosita."

Barney had to work the elevator down to the ground floor, and when he got off, Mother came along behind him like a quiet, obedient child. She followed him to their apartment.

5

Snake in a Hall Tree

When they got to the apartment Mother's mood changed
again. She remembered that Barney and Rosita had
opened this locked door, and all of a sudden she wanted
to try it. She wanted to learn how. So instead of opening
her purse and getting her key, she took a brief glance up
and down the long hall, sank to her knees and stretched
out on the floor. She looked up at Barney. "Come on,"
she said, "don't get dignified now—you did it with the
cat, you can do it with me. Come on, show me."

Barney stretched out beside his mother. Together they
fingertipped the door and pushed up. It sprang open, but
by the time it thudded against the wall, Mother had
jumped up.

"All right, now I can do it too. Now we'll go and look for Rosita. It's the only way we're going to get her for you."

Barney was brave now he had someone with him. He raised his hand and knocked on the first white door next to their own.

The door was flung open so quickly it seemed as if someone had been waiting there. A woman stood wide in the doorway, her arms at her sides as if she had to stop Mother and Barney from coming in.

Barney was struck dumb, even Mother was startled. She stammered, "There was a white cat, sort of like a rabbit, and we . . ."

"Cat! Rabbit! I don't want either one. They don't allow pets here. No salesmen either. Didn't you read my sign? I'll read it for you." She pointed to a tiny sign on the door and read in a loud, forbidding voice: "NO SALES-MEN, NO SOLICITORS."

The words on the sign were small, but she read them in big capital letters, then she slammed the door shut.

Barney and Mother looked at each other. Instead of making Mother angry it seemed as if the door's slam had slammed all her homesickness away. Like that, Mother changed from being sad and once more was mischievous. She promptly rang the woman's bell above the sign, then when nothing happened, she softly tick-rapped her

fingers up and down the door. It sounded more like rat
scratchings than any kind of a knock. It must have made
the woman curious for the door flew open, and there she
stood.

"It's us again," Mother told her meekly. "You mistook
what we said. We've nothing to sell, we were looking for
a cat. But we're both worried—won't your door close
softly?"

The woman's face fell in surprise. "I don't know," she
said worriedly.

"Shouldn't we try it?" Mother asked.

The woman stepped back and softly closed the door.

Barney and his mother couldn't keep the giggles back.
They ran for the elevator and their giggles trailed on behind them.

On the elevator Barney became sober. "Mother," he
said, "if Rosita went into an apartment with nobody
there but a dog . . ."

"You do have the nicest ideas!" Mother laughed at
him. "Why don't you think big if you want to scare yourself, why not an alligator or a crocodile?"

Barney laughed doubtfully and shivered a little.
Mother sure was feeling wild on her free afternoon. *He*
was worried.

"Look," Mother told him, "if we knock and nobody
comes, I'll make rickety-tickety noises on the door and if

Rosita is inside she'll surely come to the door and I can wriggle my fingers under it and if a white paw shoots out, well, there's your Rosita. Then we can open the door. Okay?"

"But watch out for a biting dog," Barney warned. "Don't stick your fingers through too far—you're just learning."

"Yes, master," Mother said meekly, and suddenly hugged him.

At their first door on the seventh floor nothing happened, nobody came. "Still, there's something inside," Mother said. "It's scary here, I can feel it." She pushed Barney back and dropped to her knees and pulled up on the door. It didn't open at once and when Barney started to kneel down to help her, she made him go back. "There's something strange here," she whispered. "I can feel it, I feel shivery. It could be someone needing help, but I don't know. I've got to see. I won't go in, I'll just look and call." As she said it she dropped down and pushed the tips of her fingers under the door. This time it came open easily.

Inside the entrance hall there rose a rough sort of clothes tree that reached to the ceiling. In the dimness Barney saw something peel off the cross branches of the wooden tree. It flowed like water down the main trunk of the hall tree and slid toward the door. It was a snake!

Barney leaped forward, pushed Mother aside and slammed the door shut as the snake slithered toward her. Mother got up slowly. She shook her head. "The pets some people keep," she whispered. But when she saw how scared Barney was she made a quick little joke. "Some keep rabbits, some keep snakes," she said.

"Oh, he was big!" Barney said shakily. "He was as thick around as I am! Big enough to crush all your ribs!" He felt his ribs. "He must be a boa constrictor."

"Oh, now, Barney," Mother laughed, "it wasn't a monster. I saw it too. But it does mean we open no more doors, no matter what queer feelings I get."

They stood in the middle of the hall, well away from the door. Still looking back they went to the elevator and down to their own apartment. Mother started rummaging in her purse for her key. "Oh, well, it's safe to open our own door Rosita's way."

Mother got down on the floor but Barney had a sudden ghastly thought. "Mother, that door opened so easy—what if Rosita went in there and the snake came down from the tree and wrapped itself around her and crushed her . . . and . . . swallowed her whole!"

Mother looked up at him and laughed right out. "Rosita inside a snake! More likely our goldfish are inside Rosita, if she came back while we were away."

But Barney wouldn't laugh. Scared as he was he could only stay stubborn. He bent down to whisper, "You saw the snake close when he slid over the floor, was there a lump in his middle?"

"Barney!" Mother was so startled by the thought that she whispered too. "Stop that nonsense. Come help me open this door, and let's get inside and sit down calmly."

There was nothing to do but stretch out and help open the door. Barney put his fingertips beside Mother's.

The door opened before they'd hardly touched it, and there stood Barney's father. He must have just started to come out of the door, for he almost stepped on them. He looked down at them.

They looked up at him.

"I thought I heard whispers out here," he said. He shook his head. "Now I guess I've seen everything. My whole family stretched upside down on the floor of a public hallway." He came forward, stooped and looked in their faces. "What are you doing down there?" he asked in a gentle way as if he'd made up his mind that both of them had gone crazy and must be handled calmly.

Mother rolled over, and as she scrambled back to her feet she nudged Barney. "Say something!" she hissed.

But Barney was speechless. He tried to say something sensible but he couldn't. Everything seemed to wait. Then his words came in a rush.

"Dad, Dad, we saw a great big snake. Mother and I learned how to open doors from a cat, but when we did open a door there was a snake, and he'd swallowed our cat. It was a boa constrictor."

"Oh, a boa constrictor," Father said feebly. "Well now, of course, that explains everything. And that's why you're both on the floor—you're seeing snakes. Yes, that makes everything clear."

Barney jumped up. Maybe he could say things better standing up. Mother was on her feet too, and she said, "The more you say, the worse it gets." Then she said very politely to her husband, "May we come in? You're sort of blocking the doorway." She said it with great dignity. "If I can come in and sit down, maybe I can explain. It's really quite natural."

"Oh, that I can readily believe," Father said, and stepped aside.

Mother went by him into the living room and plumped down on the low stool beside the goldfish, but then all she did was to stare at the fish bowl. Father came in and stood before her and stared down. Barney dribbled after them and all was silent.

"Rosita is a cat," Barney started, but Father just stared down at Mother.

"Rosita is a cat," he tried again, "and she came in here —she just opened the door, and came in. She pushes up on the door with her paws, and the lock unclicks and the door comes open. She came in that way and she went out that way and that showed me how to do it, and I showed Mother."

"A cat showed you how to open doors?" Father said slowly.

"Yes," Barney said, and Mother nodded. "But," Barney added, "when Rosita—that's the cat—left here, she opened a door and went into another apartment and a snake got her. It was a boa constrictor and he was as big around, oh, as big around as Mother's leg, and as long as a river."

"A *big* boa constrictor," Father agreed. "Now you go get me a *big* glass of cold water."

Looking at him, Barney ran. He let the water run in the kitchen sink, and filled the glass at least twenty times, then he heard laughing in the living room. Now it was safe. He brought the water to his father. It must be that everything was settled nicely without him, for as Dad took the cold water he smiled at him and asked, "Did you find your Rosita?"

Barney shook his head bleakly. "She's in the snake," he said.

"Well," Father said, "something will have to be done about that. A cat like Rosita you don't find every day, nor even every other day, and your mother is sure the cat's not in the snake, because she's sure the snake isn't half as big around as her leg, in fact, only about as thick as her wrist."

Mother held up her wrist. Barney grinned gratefully and said, "I guess he got bigger and bigger the scareder I made myself."

"I was guessing that too," Dad agreed. Then he stopped being friendly and got businesslike. He pulled out the big old-fashioned watch Grandpa had given him the day they left. He looked at it, snapped it shut, and stood up. "Well, shall we go?" he asked Mother. "We've got to go," he told Barney, "if we're going to save our jobs. But tonight I promise you we'll help you hunt Rosita."

"But what if I don't want to go back to that job?" Mother said.

"Then we're both out of a job."

"Oh, no," Mother said. "How do you know?"

"They called me from your office and told me. They said if you had a good excuse for running off like that, they'd take you back."

"But why should you lose your job because of me?"

"I suppose they thought that would bring you back. They said managers were a dime for two dozen, but good bookkeeper-buyers were hard to find."

Mother looked pleased. "If I was that good, why didn't they tell me so?" she demanded.

"They've said it now—in their way," Dad said. "All right, come on, let's get back before closing time."

"Well! if I'm *that* important," Mother said proudly. She got up and walked to the entry.

"Are you just going?" Barney wailed. "With Rosita still gone?"

Mother was starting to pick up her purse, but at Barney's yelp, she straightened. "That's right!" she told Dad. "I can't go back with that cat still gone. I know exactly what Barney's going to do. The moment we're gone, he'll go and look for his cat—even out in the streets and alleys if necessary."

"He wouldn't," Dad said determinedly. "And he won't. After we get home I'll help him find his cat."

"But, Dad," Barney wailed, "you come home so late! That'll be hours, and Rosita's already been gone for hours."

"Just the same, promise me that . . ." Dad started to say.

"Promise!" Mother shook her head. "Do you know Barney's been up on the roof—seven stories up?"

"On the roof?" Dad exploded.

"Yes, on the roof for that cat."

"You don't suppose," Barney hastily spoke up, "that Rosita's gone back to the roof? We've been here a long time, and . . ."

"I suppose that you're getting a little too smart," Dad interrupted him. "You know just how to get your mother upset enough so she won't go back. But you're going to stay here—and alone. Do you want us to lose our jobs over a cat?"

"Mother doesn't mind," Barney said stoutly. "Mother wants to go home, and so do I."

"But I'd feel like a fool, going back," Father said. "A failure! Back home to the village in just one week—dismissed, fired! Now do you want to promise me you'll stay here, or do you want me to lose my job?"

"Promise," Barney whispered hoarsely.

"All right, then," Dad said, jerked the door open, and pushed Mother ahead of him into the hall.

6

The Flower Cat

Barney's father jerked the door open and pushed Mother through so suddenly that nobody saw the tall, skinny, stringy young man standing there with his hand raised to knock. The young man, taken by surprise, knocked on Mother instead of the door. With a startled squeak Mother jumped back.

The young man's hair hung below his shoulders and was held away from his face by a broad ribbon band. Around his neck were strung odd shapes of big beads, and his pants—Barney's eyes grew big—the pants had red roses printed all over them!

"It's a hippie, Dad," he whispered.

Father demanded, "What do you want? What can we do for you?"

"What do I want, man?" the hippie said indignantly. "I just wanted to sell a cat—not knock on a woman. Do you two always come out of doors that way?"

"A cat?" Barney asked. "A white cat?"

The hippie swung a knapsack on his back around to his front, and opened it. Out of the narrow knapsack top popped a white rabbity head, out of the whole knapsack rose an indignant white cat. It was Rosita!

Rosita wasn't in the boa constrictor, Rosita was in a knapsack. She clawed her way out, but the hippie grabbed her and held her clenched in his arms.

"It's Rosita," Barney said. "It's my cat!"

"Your cat!" the hippie said. "Can't you see she's mine, man?" His black beard bristled with indignation, and he nuzzled Rosita to show that she was his. "I'm here to sell her, is all," he told Mother out of Rosita's white fur. "Why not buy her for the kid to teach him to love all animals?" He nudged his hairy head in Barney's direction. "It'll do him good—he acts too smart."

"That would be fine," Father said ominously, "but you see the kid already has a cat, and from the way he described her to me, I'd say your cat is his cat."

"Is this your cat?" Dad asked Barney right before the hippie.

Barney nodded, too much taken aback by the hippie's cool nerve to be able to say much of anything. Affronted, he stared up at the tall, skinny hippie, for Rosita was rubbing her white fur along the hippie's whole messy black beard.

Rosita did not even look at Barney. She didn't act one little bit as if she knew him, or had eaten half his hot dogs. Oh, she was a contrary cat, always doing the last thing you expected of her.

"So the kid told you she was his," the hippie said slowly. "Sure, in a way she is anybody's cat, she's that friendly, but she belongs to me. Lives with me in the basement—I'm helping the janitor out. It's dirty down there, so she keeps going upstairs. She's smart—knows enough to keep moving because no cats are allowed in this building. No cats, no dogs and no children!" He nudged his pointed beard toward Barney. "So what's he doing here? How come you keep a kid here?"

"Oh, we keep moving him around too," Mother said for a joke, but only she and Barney laughed. "You see, he's our child, not our kid, and he lives with us," Mother informed the hippie sweetly.

"Yeah, it's best to keep moving around—the cat, too," the hippie said earnestly. "The landlord is a . . ." He looked at Mother. "The landlord is a so-and-so," he said too mildly. "You can take my word."

"No cats, no dogs, no children?" Father suddenly asked. "How about snakes?"

"You mean snaky snakes, man?" the hippie asked back. Then he shrugged. "I wouldn't know—snakes aren't my bag."

Dad suddenly stooped to Barney. "At least you know your Rosita isn't in the snake," he said softly out of the side of his mouth.

Barney nodded.

"But it looks to me she isn't much better off," Dad said a little behind one hand. "He looks skinny enough to eat her some day."

Mother must have been afraid the hippie could hear, for she hastily asked him, "Did you say no children in this apartment building?"

"Absolutely not! I don't know how it is you're getting away with it," the hippie told her.

"I guess we didn't ask when we rented this, so we didn't know," Mother said.

"Better not let the landlord catch you. He'll tell you you have to put the kid in the trash can," the hippie warned, and for the first time grinned and seemed to feel at ease. His smiling mouth was a red moist slit inside his black beard. "The cat's not allowed either, but she keeps on the move and hides better." He grinned out at Mother. "If you buy the cat, I'll take the kid out to the trash cans in the alley for you." The black beard opened and he grinned at Barney.

Barney poked out his tongue and grinned back at him.

"Well, what do you say?" The hippie glanced up the hall and got businesslike. "Do you want this flower cat for three dollars? Is that too much for a cat with three round daisy marks plain around her ring tail on her white hide?"

"What's a flower cat?" Barney demanded.

The hippie held Rosita down for him to see. "See the ring tail? She must have got that from a raccoon. Somewhere a raccoon got mixed up in all this. But that's not important—see those three round spots right around where her tail starts up—those are daisies, and that's what makes her a flower cat. Get it? Understand? It's as near to daisies as you can get on a cat. What do you want —sunflowers?"

"Rosita!" Barney said right into her shell-pink ear. "When she was mine I called her Rosita," he explained to the hippie. Rosita did not turn her head, she acted as if she had never eaten hot dogs with him. Clenched tight in the hippie's long skinny hands, she only looked pained and distant.

"Rosita?" the hippie said. "Well, it is a name, man— and you've got to call them something. I call her Celess."

"Celeste, you mean," Mother corrected.

"No, Celess!" the hippie insisted. "I hate names with
't's. I hate to have to cross 't's."

"How are you with 'i's and their dots?" Dad asked
him, amused.

"They're even worse, man. Who can remember to
crown 'i's with their dots? What's a dot to bother with? I
was going to take a trip down the Mississippi once, but
I gave it up—too many 'i's to dot on the postcards you'd
send your friends from that river. I've decided there's
only one river that I want to go down. That's the Po
River in Europe. For all I know it may not flow—that
generation of yours may have made it a sewer—but there
is a river that spells itself." He was so busy talking and at
the same time trying to keep Rosita from twisting out of
his hands that Barney could keep stroking Rosita and
whispering to her. "Rosita," he whispered. "Rosita."

At last Rosita responded, and listened, snaked out of
the hippie's hands, and stepped onto Barney's shoulder.
She rubbed her white cheek against Barney's cheek, and
sang him a snug little song of pure happiness. Barney
couldn't help grinning up at the hippie. "See? See?" he
said. "She *is* my cat."

"She's yours if your dad gives me three dollars," the
hippie said promptly. "If not I might have to report that
your dad and mother keep a kid here. I need three dollars."

But to show he was sort of half joking, the hippie showed all his white teeth in a wide grin, and he looked straight into Dad's eyes.

To Barney's and Mother's amazement Dad poked in his back pocket and came out with his billfold, and then stood fingering three one-dollar bills. He held them out to the hippie, but at the same time he pulled Barney with his Rosita back from the doorway. "There—there's your three," he said to the hippie, after he'd first looked behind him to see that Barney was well back and still holding Rosita.

"Thanks, man, thanks," the hippie said sort of astounded. He looked at the three bills in his hand, whirled on his heels and ran so hard for the outer door the empty knapsack bobbed and flapped against his narrow, stooped back.

"What is it with you?" Mother exploded to Dad, once the hippie was gone. "Rosita was no more his cat than she is Barney's, and you know it."

"Sure, man," Father said like the hippie, and laughed. "Sure, I know it, but buying her makes her feel much more ours, and our thin man can use a square meal—if he'll eat anything that is square. I had to get rid of him, if we're going to get back to your office."

Already Dad had his watch out of his pocket. He looked at it as he stepped out into the hall. "Okay," he told Mother, "if we don't find a taxi you and I'll have to run if we're going to make it." He started to close the door. "Bye, Barney, be a good boy, now that you've got a good three-dollar cat. Bye, Rosita—the *kid* isn't bad either."

Outside Mother laughed, but Father firmly closed the door in Barney's and Rosita's faces.

Inside, Barney stood grinning but then Mother called out, "Oh, Barney, in all this fuss, I forgot my purse. Your father's already way down the hall. Hand it to me, will you?"

Barney threw Rosita across his shoulder and ran to get the purse, but as he held it out to Mother through the partly open door, Rosita jumped over both their arms and streaked away down the hall.

Barney leaped past Mother. "Dad, Dad!" he screamed. "Watch it, Rosita's got out! Rosita's coming. Catch her!"

Down the hall Father whirled to intercept Rosita but she flattened and slid from under his hand and tore on.

Just then a lady who had stepped on the elevator poked her head out of the door to see what was going on, but the door snake-slid itself shut and caught her shoulders. She twisted free, but lost her balance, stumbled out of the elevator and fell flat on her face in the hall. The panicked Rosita, running toward her, leaped over her into the elevator just as the door hissed shut.

It was so close that the white hairs on the tip of Rosita's tail got cut off by the closing door. The tuft of hair floated peacefully on a draft through the long hall. The stunned woman, now up on her knees, watched the wafting tuft as if hypnotized.

Behind the closed door Rosita was riding the elevator up by herself to whatever floor the woman may have punched when she had first gotten on. There the elevator would open to let Rosita out, free to go anywhere.

Barney and Father and Mother all thought of it at the same time, and all three from different directions charged toward the bewildered woman, down on her knees, watching the white tuft of hair that was the outermost tip of Rosita's ring tail.

7

No Cats Allowed

Father got to the fallen woman first. He helped her up, but even as he helped her to her feet, he was asking her, "What floor were you going to?"

"It was—it was the fifth," the woman told Father. She acted suspicious. "Why do you want to know? Of course, the fifth—I live on the fifth with my kitty."

"A white cat with a ring tail?" Barney shouted.

The woman's face closed as she saw Barney's mother also come running up. "I live on the fifth," she said firmly. "And I don't have a white kitten—cats aren't allowed here." She turned to Mother. "Wouldn't you say odd things when you'd just fallen on your face and saw a big man pounding down on you?"

"I guess I would," Mother assured her. "Yes, I would!"
she said indignantly, and past the woman grinned wick-
edly at Father. "But you see the reason we were running
so hard was because even though there aren't supposed
to be cats in this building, the three of us just saw a white
cat jump over you into the elevator. Now we have to
know which floor you were going to, because that's where
the cat's going in place of you, and that's where she'll get
off."

"Then I won't tell you," the woman mumbled. She
suddenly hurried down the hall and picked the floating
tuft of hair out of the air. She looked at it, shook her head
and said, "No, it isn't tawny, it's white, so it wasn't *my*
kitty." Then she turned on all three of them and said,
"But I won't say one thing more."

As she said it they all whirled at a hissing sound behind
them. The elevator had come back to the main floor.
Its door was sighing open, but nothing came out. When
they all crowded in, there was nothing inside. Rosita was
gone.

The woman pushed one of the elevator buttons. "Do
you want to come along?" she then asked.

"If the button you punched is to the floor where the
cat went, oh, yes," Mother said. "Oh, absolutely."

Then they rode up in silence, but when the elevator
stopped, and its door opened, they weren't on the fifth
floor as the woman had said—they had stepped out onto

the seventh and highest floor, the floor under the roof, the floor of the apartment with the boa constrictor.

While they stood looking up and down the long hall for Rosita, the woman disappeared, then somewhere a door slammed. They ran, but when they came around the corner there was no white cat—and no woman. There was no guessing which apartment the woman had entered, so while Dad and Mother waited, Barney raced around the four halls, but there was no Rosita anywhere.

They stood puzzled. "Now why did that woman tell us the fifth floor when it plainly was the seventh?" Dad muttered. "Well, I guess that leaves us only one thing to do, begin at the door next to Barney's boa constrictor, and ask at every door. But this time without opening them!"

"After that snake, what do you think?" Mother indignantly said. "But come on, let's get started."

Barney was as amazed as she that Father had so easily agreed to go from door to door to look for Rosita. It must be Father had amazed himself, for he suddenly pulled out his watch. "All right," he said, "but just this one floor! We know she's got to be here somewhere, so if we each take a door we can do it fast and still have time to get back to the office."

Mother and Barney gave him no chance to change his mind. Each raced to a door and let Father take the nearest one. Behind them they heard him rap, but he'd pounded so hard in his hurry that the door sprang open,

and out of the doorway something white came hurling
as if shot from a catapult. Like a missile it thudded
against Dad so hard that he flung his arms around it, and
staggered back against the wall.

"Dad," Barney screamed, "Dad, it's a kangaroo!"

A woman came rushing out. "Thank goodness, you've
got him," she gasped. Then she looked at Father and the
animal. "Oh, don't hold him that way—turn him around!
If he kicks, he'll disembowel you!"

"Disembowel me!" Dad yelled. He hurled the beast
backward across the hall. The woman caught it neatly
but its weight sent her staggering. She ended on a white
bench in her entryway. The kangaroo sat on her lap.

"Well," she said when she got her breath back, "that
wasn't a very gentlemanly thing to do—heave a wallaby
at a lady."

Dad got red and looked upset at what he'd done.
"Well," he said, "I'll be . . . so that's what it is—a wallaby.
I'm sorry for what I did, but I hate to be disemboweled
in public, so I just tossed him."

"What is it?" Mother asked. "Where'd you ever get
him?"

"Just down the street at a fancy pet store. You can buy
all sorts of animals from everywhere there. Nearly everybody up here on the seventh floor has got some kind

of odd pet they bought there. You see, we have to keep sort of out-of-the-way beasties for pets—just so it isn't a cat or a dog—because cats and dogs absolutely aren't allowed in this building. It says so right out in so many words in the lease when you rent an apartment here."

"But what is it?" Mother asked again.

"It's a white wallaby from Australia. They grow all kinds of strange animals there—kangaroos and koala bears and platypuses and boomerangs . . ."

"You throw a boomerang! It's not an animal," Barney told her.

"Oh, sonny, I'm glad to know that," she said. "I thought when they talked about throwing a boomerang it was like us talking about throwing the bull. A bull is an animal. . . . But you three aren't here to spy for the landlord, are you?" she demanded abruptly. "You're here with a boy, and children aren't allowed to live here any-more than housecats or dogs. It says so right out in the lease, but the lease doesn't mention wallabies, so there! Anyway, everybody who keeps pets lives up here on the seventh floor, because the landlord won't come higher than the sixth. You ought to see the queer pets!" She shuddered. "One man even keeps a snake. He says it likes to be stroked, says that it isn't slimy, but dry like a cork." She shuddered again.

Barney's mind was on the wallaby. "How far can your wallaby jump?" he asked. "Bet it can jump anyway twenty feet!"

"All I know is that in twenty-three jumps it gets around these four halls. I counted! But I can't leap twenty feet—I have to run. That's why I keep this bench here. I have to sit down when I've caught him."

"May I hold him?" Barney begged. "Can I pet him?"

"Why, sure," the woman said. "Sit down here but keep his hind feet away from you—if you don't want to be disemboweled," she said with a grin for Father.

Barney sat down. The baby wallaby nuzzled his face. He rubbed his furry white head along Barney's cheek and looked up at him with big liquid eyes. "You don't have a cat too, do you?" he asked. "A white, rabbity cat?"

"No. No cats are allowed," the woman said. She looked at Mother. "You said you live here—you have a child, how come?"

"Well . . ." Mother started, but Father stopped her by holding up his watch.

"After today," he told the woman, "we won't be living here. After today we won't be living anywhere—we'll be out of work." He put the watch back in his pocket. "It was nice meeting you and your very sudden wallaby, but we've got to hurry now."

The friendly woman sighed. "Everybody is in such a hurry, nobody has time for anything. It gets lonely. If my wallaby could only talk . . ."

Father had hurried out and Barney followed. Mother stayed behind to say some apologetic parting things. Then she came.

Barney went to the last door around the corner in the end hall. It turned out to be the apartment of the woman who'd fallen out of the elevator.

"I thought you'd come," she said. But now she wasn't confused, now she was friendly. "Did you find your white cat? No? Well, now you're here why don't you come in and see Kitty. Come in and scratch his belly for him—he loves it. It makes him roar."

"Roar?" Barney asked. She must be crazy! He was glad Mother and Dad were coming around the corner.

"May my mother and dad see him too?" he asked.

"Oh, are they here too? Well, let's have Kitty come to the door. Kitty, Kitty, Kitty," she called. "Come meet the nice people." Nothing came, but when they peered past the woman, there before the window on a table lay a tawny lion cub.

"I thought, I thought . . ." Barney backed away until he stepped on his father's toes. "You called it 'Kitty,'" he accused.

"You mayn't have cats in the building," she answered, "but I wanted one so bad that I call my lion Kitty. Kitty, Kitty," she called out again. But the little lion didn't come.

"I'm afraid you'll have to go in to him. Kitty is a little shy, but once you've scratched him on his little round belly, he'll always remember you."

The three of them came toward the table. The little lion heard them and turned over with a big wide yawn, put his paws in the air and held his little belly ready.

The old lady nudged Barney. "Go on, don't be afraid. He likes children."

"To eat?" Barney grinned half ashamed, and stretched out one hand so only his fingertips just touched the lion. The little lion opened his jaws in another great yawn that to Barney looked wide as an ocean full of white teeth. Tired of waiting, the cub scrubbed his head against the corner of the table to scratch himself somewhere, if nobody was going to do it for him.

"The poor thing is glad to see somebody new," the woman said. "He never gets out of this room."

"Never?" Barney asked. "Never outdoors?"

"All he sees is what he sees from this window," the woman told him.

Then Barney felt so sorry he wasn't afraid any longer. He started rubbing the little lion's belly and the little cub lay on his back, paws in the air, his head turned adoringly to the boy who was scratching him. His silly red rag of a tongue lolled out of his mouth in his delight, and he moaned and groaned and crooned like a baby. Finally he was so happy he raised his head and roared a baby roar.

It was so sweet and wonderful that Mother had to scratch the little cub too, and he moaned out his ecstasy to her. Mother and Barney got in each other's way, then Dad crowded between them. "My turn now," he said, "out of my way, you two. It's my turn. How many times do you get a chance to play with a lion?"

With nothing to do but stand and watch Dad playing with the little lion, Barney couldn't resist. He *had* to hold a lion, he had to hug the little lion, paws up, in his arms. He squeezed in beside Dad and lifted the lion from the table. The little upside-down lion stretched his head so that it rested on Barney's shoulder and while Mother and Dad were still petting him, he slobbered his red-rag wet tongue all over Barney's face and up through his hair. Mother and Dad tickled the little lion until he could stand it no longer—it was too much to endure. He threw himself up over Barney's shoulder to get away from it. And then, like Rosita, he rubbed his cheek and hairy, tickling chin against Barney's face, and burbled into Barney's ear.

Barney burbled back to him, but then *he* could take it no more—it was too much. "Oh, Mom, oh, Dad! If I could have a lion like him!" He knew they couldn't give him a lion. But the words just broke out of him—it was too much, he didn't know what to do from sheer excitement and joy.

Suddenly it was sad. He shoved the lion into Dad's arms and ran. He ran straight to the stairway to be up on the roof where everything was wide and the sky was above him.

Barney stood crying. Alone, he cried unashamedly. Love, happiness and hopeless longing to have the baby lion were all mixed together. He couldn't have the lion, he knew it.

It was good that right then his father's head came pushing up through the trap door from the stairway and his voice said quietly, "Barney, you couldn't even hope it."

"Yes, I know," Barney choked out, and was crying again.

Dad wasn't ashamed of him. "That's all you can do—cry it out. I could cry myself, that lion was such a honey. But his lady loves him, and he's all she has. You have us and when we find her you'll have your Rosita. Come on, Son, let's go down and get Mother. She's visiting with an old lady that's sick."

He handed Barney his handkerchief. "Here, give a good blow, you'll feel better."

Barney rubbed his eyes dry. "Dad," he said, "before you go down, please, look out there—there's our river."

Then he quickly ran down the stairs so that his father would be alone. At the foot he waited but Dad stayed up there. He must have wanted to be alone.

Down the hall came the faint sound of voices. He went to look for his mother.

8

Hold a Lion

Barney stood hesitating at the open door of the apartment where he'd heard Mother's voice, not knowing whether he should go into a room where a woman was sick, not knowing if he should knock at an open door. Then luckily Father came down from the roof. But to Barney's surprise and disappointment, his father looked grim. Seeing the river and hills hadn't made Father homesick, the way it had him and Mother—it seemed to have made him serious and grim.

Dad had his watch in his hand. Without saying a word he showed the time on the watch to Barney. "Maybe there's still time to get back to that office," he announced loudly. "But just time and no more."

Mother, inside the room, heard him and came to them at the door. Dad showed her the watch, but she didn't look at it, she only looked stubborn. "She's in there alone, waiting to go to the hospital, and she's very sick. I've got to help her," she told Dad firmly.

Father didn't seem to have heard. "It's one thing to quit, it's another to be miserably fired," he said. "It means you've failed."

"Not having failed means a lot to you, doesn't it?" Mother said. "If it's that important, we'll go to the office, but I've got to help her now. I knocked but she is so sick, she couldn't come to the door, she called me from her bed. I went in, and now I've got to help, and that is important to me!"

Dad grunted, and shoved his watch in his pocket. "Well, then we're fired," he said with a hopeless shrug.

For a moment Mother looked helpless, but she said, "Couldn't you call in and say that you've quit? Couldn't you pick up the phone and say in so many words: 'Mister President of the Lucky Boy Grocery Company, I'm not coming back because I have quit. And my wife has quit too. So goodbye, and all kinds of luck to you and your corporation, but we're going home.' Couldn't you just do that?"

"It isn't honorable not to go down and face them," Father said stiffly, "face the music. But I can tell you right now, it would give me great pleasure to do just what you said—great pleasure!"

Inside himself Barney cheered for his father, but was hoping Mother would win. Then the sick woman called out from her bed, and they all turned. The old lady was sitting up in her bed, stringy hair hanging around her thin face, but she told Mother, "Your men folks may come in. All of you *do* come in! Oh, I knew somebody would come in time, I've prayed all day. I can manage to get myself ready for the hospital some way, but I've prayed all day that somebody would come in time to save my cat. And now you have come."

"Of course we've come," Mother said, and hurried back in. Barney and Dad doubtfully followed her. Dad didn't seem to know either whether it was proper for a man and a boy to come into the sickroom of a sick woman. The little wisp of a woman lay back, breathing hard, and Mother ordered, "Don't try to talk. We'll help you."

The little old lady raised her head just the same, and she said, "It isn't I that needs help in the first place—it's my white cat! I'm going to the hospital—they're coming for me any minute—that landlord with them, so first I've got to take care of my Pinky. Otherwise the landlord will take her to the animal pound."

"Pinky?" Barney ran to the bed. "Did you say Pinky? Is your Pinky white with a ring tail and three round spots? Because that's *my* Rosita."

The old lady smiled up at him. "That's *my* Pinky too, so she's the same cat. But now she'll be your cat, not mine any more. All day long, all I could, I've been keeping my door wide open, hoping that someone somewhere in this building would take her in when I go to the hospital. The landlord said he'd take care of me—I'm his oldest tenant, I've been here since the building was built—but he wouldn't take care of my cat. He hates cats and they scare him. But now you will save her, and have your Rosita that's my Pinky. You are the people, I know it." She lay back exhausted, but still whispered to Barney, "It's not only Rosita-Pinky's ring tail and spots, but did you notice her see-through pink ears, and that pink nose bud of hers—and the pink pads on those paws?"

Barney nodded and nodded. "That's why I called her Rosita," he told her, amazed. "Did you know that Rosita can open doors?"

"Yes, I taught her," the old lady said. "Yesterday when I still had the strength to crawl to the door, I taught her, and today I kept my door open so she could go anywhere and maybe open somebody's door and go in—then they'd find her and love her and keep her."

"Then is she here?" Mother asked.

"Oh, no, not here! This is the last place she should be with the landlord coming. I don't know where she is, but it's most important that she isn't here. The landlord would take her to the pound."

"Do you really think so?" Mother said. "Everybody seems so afraid of this landlord, but do you really think he'd do that?"

"I know so," the old lady said. "You see, I'm the landlord's mother. That's how I knew these locks were defective, and how the doors could be opened, so I taught Rosita."

"The landlord's mother!" Dad said in amazement, and stood shaking his head.

"The landlord's your son?" Mother said after him like an echo.

"The landlord's own mother?" Barney said in astonishment.

"His very own!" The sick little old lady laughed. "I can laugh now," she said sweetly contented, "because you are here, and you'll find Barney's Rosita, and keep her. And it's right—because I am old and going to the hospital, but Barney is young and Rosita is young, and they will live long together. But, Barney, you must send me a card in the hospital telling me just how you found her, and all about Rosita and you. Is that a promise? Because if it is, then Rosita is yours."

Barney was speechless. Father spoke up for him. "I'll see to it," he said. "You know how boys are about writing, but I'll see that he writes you a card every day."

"So will I," Mother said.

The little old lady thanked them with her eyes. Then they all were still. In the stillness they heard a siren down in the street, moments later there came a sudden hard pounding on the frame of the sick woman's open door.

It was the lion lady from down the hall. There she stood, her little lion in her arms, and shrieked out at them, "The ambulance is down in the street, and they're coming up here with a stretcher, but the landlord is with them! If the landlord's coming up here, what will I do with Kitty?" She whirled toward a noise she must have heard down the hall, then ran into the room, shoved the lion at Barney, and wildly pleaded, "Run. You've got young legs and can run and hide him. Hide him for me from that landlord."

She didn't wait, but scuttled away to her room, and Dad in his surprise ran after her. But Barney turned to the bed. "What can I do? Where will I hide him?" he asked as wildly as the lion lady had asked him.

"Why, up on the roof—up on the roof," the sick woman said. "My son wouldn't go there for all the money there is in the world. Don't worry, I won't give it away. Nobody on this whole floor knows that I am the landlord's mother, because with all their lions and wallabies and pets, I never gave them away to my son. But you can't blame my son for not liking heights and hating cats

—a cat clawed and bit him when he was little, and to get away from the cat, he fell out of a window. He fell through three awnings and they broke his fall, but he still limps, and since then all his life he's been afraid of cats and of heights."

Father was back. "I can't make her come to the door," he announced. "She must think I'm the landlord."

"Run with Barney," the old lady urged. "And, Barney, good luck, and God bless, and do write me about Rosita. Now run."

But as Barney ran from the door with the lion, down the hall the elevator door opened, and a wheeled stretcher came poking out, a big man limped out, and two men in white were wheeling the stretcher. The man in black must be the landlord.

"Dad!" Barney hissed out. "The stretcher, the landlord —they're here."

But Dad pushed him on, pushed himself in behind Barney and the lion to block them from view of the men down the hall. Then Barney with his arms full of lion couldn't open the stairway door, but Dad silently reached around him, got the door open and shoved Barney through.

Behind the shut door they waited and listened, hoping against hope the landlord had not seen the lion. At last through the door came the landlord's big voice making clumsy, babying, comforting talk to his sick mother. And Mother talked, talked and talked, it must be, to distract the landlord in case he had noticed anything in the hall.

Then Barney and Dad stole up the stairs, and at the top Father reached past Barney and pushed the trap door up on the roof without making a sound. And there was Rosita! There jumped Rosita!

Rosita must have been sunning herself on the warm, wooden trap door, and Dad had turned her over with the door. On the top step Barney nudged and nudged his head to point out Rosita to Dad, too excited to talk. But from the roof Rosita saw the lion rising with Barney, and flew to the outer edge of the roof and its knee-high wall. That gave Barney his voice. He jumped out of Dad's way, and yelled, "Dad, Dad, catch her! It's seven stories down. Dad, catch her!"

He dashed after Rosita himself, the best he could with the lion. He couldn't let go of a cub lion with no sense at all about the outdoors—the little lion would surely go over the wall.

The lion in Barney's arms saw the streaking cat. He yelped his delight, he quivered, he wanted the cat. There was no holding him. He seemed suddenly all loose skin, he stripped out of Barney's arms, and stormed after Rosita. He was ten times faster than she, and ten times bigger. He must have seemed enormous to the terrified cat.

Just before the knee-high wall he headed her off. He only wanted to nose her and lick her and play and be friends—she was another cat! Desperately Rosita threw herself back, flipped completely over, and tore for the open trap door and the stairway. Dad was in the way. Before Rosita rose Dad, and that moment he must have seemed the highest, safest thing to her that rose from the flat roof. She sailed to Dad's shoulder, from there to his head, and there she dug in, clawing and hissing desperate threats at the lion. Without hesitation, but in all baby clumsiness, he thumped full tilt up against Dad's chest, hit so hard that Father fell back against the roof's aerial. It went down and Father sat down—flat on the roof amidst its tangle. He managed to fling both his arms around the small lion. There he sat, a cat on his head, and a lion in his arms, and Rosita seemed too petrified to try to escape from her perch on his head.

Barney rushed up to pull Rosita off Father's head. "Hold it," Dad screeched. "You're scalping me. She's got all her claws down in my brain."

At that insane moment Mother poked her head out of the stairway well. "Were you calling me?" But then she took in what was happening and came running, and helped Barney. Paw by paw they had to unloosen Rosita from father's head while he held the lion down, and each white paw in turn came away with a tuft of Dad's hair. Dad rubbed his stinging head against the aerial pole that

crookedly leaned over him.

"They're gone with the stretcher," Mother said when she'd got her breath. "The landlord with them. Nobody noticed anything. . . . But you found Rosita! Or did she find you? Ah, but the landlord's mother knew we would find her, didn't she? And now she herself is on the way to the hospital."

Down below in the street the ambulance siren started. Slowly, mournfully, falteringly it began, but as the ambulance gained speed, its shriek rose to the roof. In Dad's arms the little lion began wailing back at the siren—it must hurt his ears. Rosita squeezed her head and ears away in Barney's arm, and uttered muffled cries. The shrill siren dimmed in the canyon streets and got itself lost in the sounds of the city.

Rosita's crying had made the little lion so eager to make friends, even sitting flat, Dad hardly could hold him. "Barney, do something," Dad urged. "Maybe hold Rosita by her front legs so she can't scratch, and hold her down to this little beast, else he'll pull free. He seems to want her—maybe he thinks she's his mother."

Barney did as Father said, and gingerly lowered Rosita. For some reason coming down on the lion seemed to make Rosita feel safer, and Barney could easily hold her. The little lion rumbled and bumbled his baby noises, then swiped up at Rosita with his red-rag tongue. He wriggled with delight and bubbled with love, but Rosita held herself tight, closed her eyes tight, and endured. But to everybody's amazement, the moment the baby lion pulled his tired tongue inside his mouth, Rosita reached down to his ear, purred a motherly song into it, and washed it out thoroughly. Now they were friends —washed friends.

"Mom, look!" Barney yelped out in delight. "Look, Mom."

Dad looked around too to see if Mother had seen. But Mother wasn't standing behind them. She had wandered away to the edge of the roof, she did not even hear them. There she stood at the wall as if in a dream, pointing and pointing as if to point something out to herself. Slowly she turned. "The river," she said. "The river's out there. Our river. Let's go home."

Father struggled up beside Barney. Mother came back to them as if out of her dream. No one said a word— they looked at the river.

"See our river?" Barney whispered to Rosita. "It's the river that runs past our village. It's the river Grandpa and I go fishing in."

In Dad's arms the lion pricked up his ears at Barney's whispers. But where the river went the little lion wasn't going. The wonderful baby lion wasn't going home with them—if they really were going home.

It was sad for the little city lion with only an apartment with one window to look out of. It was sad to know, but maybe it wasn't as terrible for the cub lion if he had never known the outdoors. And the lion lady loved him —had loved him so much she had thrown him at Barney to save him. Now he was saved and had to go back to her. But Rosita was going home. Barney looked at the river.

Mother must be sad-homesick too, for she suddenly said, "I don't care. Even if there is still time to go back, I don't want to go back to that office, I want to go home." She turned to Dad. "Can't we do it by phone? Can't you pick up the phone in our apartment, and say: 'Thanks for the job and the training and effort, but we've quit. We're going back home to our own little family store.' Wouldn't that be enough—and good enough even for you?"

Dad said nothing, just stood looking at the river shimmering under the hills in the evening sunshine beyond the town. But then he pulled out his watch, and tried to look at it over the wriggling lion. Dad put the watch to his ear, shook it to see if it still was running. "It can't be that late," he muttered.

The gold of the watch flickered and gleamed. With eager eyes the little lion watched it, struck out at it suddenly with a wide baby paw. The watch flew out of Dad's hand and sailed over the roof and the little low wall.

Seven stories down there was a brief shattering tinkle, and Mother started forward as if she must still save the watch. But Dad held her back, and with a strange smile on his face told her, "If you wanted to know the time, it was past six o'clock, and way past the time we could go back to the office. So we're too late, except to go home."

"Oh," Mother said. "But your watch!"

"Where we are going I won't need a watch," Father said. "Not when it's your job and your time, and your life is your own."

Suddenly Dad looked down as if he could look through the roof, and see the smashed watch through the wall. "Yeah, six o'clock, I can plainly see." He laughed a surprised laugh, and looked down as if through the roof again. "Do you know what I also see down in the basement garage of this building? I see our car. Gosh, we haven't seen it or touched it or been in it since we came. It's not only by my watch that it's time to go home."

"Let's go right now," Mother urged. "Let's not even eat one more meal in that little apartment. Let's set out, and eat on the way as we please. Let's do just what we please. Let's go."

Together they turned to the open trap door. Side by side they went to the stairway, Barney with Rosita, Dad with the lion, and Mother between. Suddenly Father raced out, and was the first down the stairs. As he opened the door at the bottom, he turned without a word and shoved the lion in Mother's arms.

"Dad," Barney gasped out, "if we're really going, can I hold the lion once more?"

But Dad had run down the hall, it must be, to get the car. Barney whirled, and held out Rosita to Mother to take the lion from her instead. Mother shook her head. "No, Barney, run down with Dad, I'll return the lion. It'll be much easier for you."

Barney looked unbelievingly at Mother.

"You knew," Mother said. "You knew he had to go back."

But Barney had held the baby lion for too long, and though he knew it would be bad, he still had to hold him for one last time. That was all he knew. He'd hoped so hard, he'd hoped so foolishly for a miracle to give him the lion, but he'd known all along—yes, he *had* known! Now the baby lion had to be held a last time.

Barney grabbed the lion from Mother and ran. He ran around all the four halls with all his might, for only by running and pounding could he run the foolish, wild hope out of him.

When he came around the last corner with the lion, Mother stood waiting for him, but waiting with her was the lion lady. Barney ran straight to her, squeezed his eyes shut and ran at her to give her the lion, but yelled out to her, "When I get back home, I'll have thirty white rabbits, but now I'll have an almost white cat to go with them."

He laughed a hard laugh. "It's funny," he yelled. "Thirty white rabbits and one rabbity cat. Isn't that funny?"

"It's funny," the lion lady agreed. "It's funny. But, Barney, my little lion is all that I have, and you saved him for me—and that's wonderful, marvelous, and *not* funny."

Barney could say nothing more, but he placed the little lion in the arms of the woman, and carefully took Rosita out of Mother's arms. He ran with her straight to the door marked STAIRWAY. But this time he ran to the stairway that led down, and he ran down all six stairways to the ground floor, and down to his own apartment. He had to run.

Dad must have gone to the basement to get the car, because nobody came when Barney knocked, so there was only one thing to do. For a last time he and Rosita lay down on the floor, and for a last time together they opened the door. The door sprang open. Rosita got up, and, ring tail up, strutted inside to the living room. The goldfish in their bowl looked out at her, and fanned their fan tails as if they were pleased.

9

Catfish Comb

The first thing Barney did when he walked into the apartment was to carry the goldfish bowl outside to the hall and set it down. Mother looked surprised. "Must they go back with us too?" she asked.

Barney nodded.

"Yes?" Mother said. "I didn't think you were that fond of them. Is it because Rosita likes to watch them?"

Barney shook his head. "They're for the river. For the next time Grandpa and I go fishing. I want to set them free."

"Ah," Mother smiled, "that's a wonderful thought. They ought to be free from this apartment too. But I don't know if they belong here or were left by the last renters, so I'll leave a dollar." She went to the table and exactly in the ring the bowl had left, she laid down a dollar bill.

Dad was already blowing their car horn in front of the apartment. Barney got their suitcases from the closet, and then Dad was at the door. "Here," Mother said to him, "you take Rosita, and, Barney, you take the goldfish and put them in the car, then pack our clothes the best you can and I'll fix a basket lunch. I don't want to stop to eat or to stay overnight. I want to go home and if we drive all night we'll be home in the morning, just before the sun comes up."

"Not quite," Father said. "It'll take a little longer but I'd like to follow the river road. We should still get there in time for Barney to go to school."

Barney knew he was teasing, and ran after his father with the goldfish. Then they were pulling the clothes out of the closet, but Dad had no patience with suitcases. "Here," he said. "Hold out your arms straight, and I'll load the clothes on them, then I'll lay them flat in the trunk. We'll toss the suitcases in the back seat. That way we'll be on our way in the jerk of a cat's tail or the flip of a fish's fin."

Barney giggled and held out his arms to let Father load.

"Be sure to take everything that's ours, but not one thing more," Mother called from the kitchen.

"You just tend to your knitting, girl. Get those sandwiches built," Father called back. "And don't forget coffee!"

"And cokes for Barney and water for Rosita," Mother mimicked.

"The goldfish have theirs," Father teased back. He must be feeling fine for he said, "Barney, do you know that if it hadn't been for Rosita, if she hadn't come opening doors, we wouldn't be going home?"

"She's a smart cat," Barney said.

Then they were ready. Then they were outside. They locked the door. It was wonderful.

The three of them rode in the front seat. They hadn't thought it out but it must be that now, going home, they needed to be close together. Barney sat in the middle with Rosita in his lap and Mother had the goldfish bowl held tight between her legs to keep it from spilling. Even so it splashed great dark splotches down her jeans. Mother told Dad that when they got beyond all the traffic, they'd better stop and arrange things a little better. Barney was thankful because he was being dug by Rosita. *She* didn't like any part of the ride, the sound of the motor or the passing swish of the cars with their piercing lights. She hated it all. She cried little whimpers of protest.

When they were leaving the city Dad said, "She'd be

better off in the back, maybe. Here she sees too much and the headlights scare her." But still he drove on and nobody said anything, because none of them wanted to take the time that was needed to change things.

Barney solved it. He handed Rosita to Father who squeezed her between himself and the steering wheel, then Barney turned around and climbed over the seat. He dropped down in the back, reached over and took the goldfish bowl and set it on the seat. Then he reached over and took Rosita.

"Would it be better to put the goldfish on the floor?" Dad asked as he watched Barney in the rear view mirror. "The seat is pretty springy." Barney shook his head and pointed.

Rosita had settled down and was all but wrapped around the bowl, her eyes on the swimming fish. Her unhappy mews had ended.

But the poor goldfish were unhappy now. Their water that had always been still now rose and fell. There was a sort of tide in their bowl, and Rosita had to keep licking to dry herself from the fine, thin splashes.

"You need a float," Dad said. "If you can find something to float in the bowl, it'll smooth out their storm."

There was nothing on the back seat but the basket of sandwiches. Barney peered into it. He could see a pickle jar and some little jars with dabs and dollops of leftovers from the refrigerator. They wouldn't help the goldfish—what could a goldfish do with a pickle jar? Then Barney looked up at the light that had come in the car and down into the basket. The moon was out! The night had come and there, right there, was the river in the moonlight. "The river! The moon's in the river," Barney shouted. Mother and Father nodded proudly as if *they* had put the moon and the river there.

Barney was so happy it made him hungry. He studied the basket again. He pulled out a sandwich to see what was in it. It was fish. He started to put it back, but Rosita jumped in his lap and sniffed. "Fish," he told her. "It's just canned fish." Rosita yammered, and when Barney started to put it back, she hooked a claw, caught the top slice and pulled it off. Plop! It fell into the goldfish bowl. He had to grab Rosita to keep her from diving after it. He gave her the other half—the half with the fish on it, and she settled to eat.

"There's a float for the fish," Barney called to Dad. "Rosita made a float for them from a slice of bread, and they're eating it."

They were. They swam up and nibbled the edges of the bread floating on top of their water.

Like that, the smell of the sandwiches filled the car and everybody was hungry. Barney handed out sandwiches as fast as he could. But he took time to find a peanut butter one for himself. He had to dig down for more and then still more, and then a last fish one for Rosita. There was nothing left but jars full of dabs and dollops. He handed the Thermos to Mother and she and Dad drank cup after cup. "It's to keep me awake on the road up the mountain," Dad said, "though if that darned moon gets any brighter, I'll need sunglasses."

Oh, it was good to be happy—and full.

Nobody talked but they all admired the river, plain as day in the moonlight. They were going home. The car rode on and on.

Later they climbed high and higher into the hills, and under the hills was the sound of their river. Inside the car was nothing but quiet happiness that home would come in the morning. It was still far away—but it would come.

Rosita, full of fish, contentedly watched the slow, gliding goldfish, full of bread. In the front seat Mother nodded, started awake and nodded again. Barney leaned his head against the basket. He tried not to sleep for he felt it wouldn't be fair to Father. If he kept awake he felt he was sort of helping twist the car up the winding road with its snake-twisty turnings. It was silly, of course, but it felt right to be doing it.

He helped so hard that from all the close staring, he fell asleep.

Barney woke with a start from what had seemed to be but two moments of sleep, and looked out of the window —straight up! He was looking at their home mountain. There it was! There in the morning sun, straight up ahead was their village, clinging to the side of its mountain. It clung there as if waiting for them to come home.

He rubbed his eyes from the sleepy thoughts and looked around. Mother was still asleep, Dad was twisting the wheel on the narrow, mountain road, Rosita was asleep, and even the fish were still.

"We're home," Barney announced.

"We're home?" Mother woke instantly.

"We're home," Dad assured them. "I just heard the school bell," he teased Barney.

Barney frowned. But then he realized Dad was feeling so happy at coming home he had to tease about school some more.

The next minute he closed his eyes to make a game so he could hold out, for he knew that up in the mountains in the clear air things looked close but might be miles away. He decided not to open his eyes until the change in the sound of the tires would tell him they had left the road, and had entered the village's one and only street. Dad's window was open, so he'd know the moment the tires were on the brick street. Every now and then he had to cheat a little—just for the blink of an eye.

The little road wrapped itself around the mountain and climbed and climbed. The river was down below and its rocky roar came up on the breeze. The river was roaring its welcome.

Then Barney made a new rule to his game. Even though he could tell they were in the village, he still might not open his eyes until they came to the barn at the end of Grandpa's drive. Then, there'd be Grandpa, he'd be the first thing they'd see!

It became hard and then harder to hang on to his own rules. But Dad mustn't stop anywhere but in front of Grandpa's barn, and Grandpa must be standing before it. Figuring out so many conditions kept him so busy that when the car did stop he let out a little squeak. The car *had* stopped before the barn and before its open door sat Grandpa. He was crouched over a fish pole, busy unsnarling a snagged line. He had his head down and he didn't even hear the car. Grandpa was a bit deaf, but he wouldn't admit it. Barney started to yell, but Mother reached back a warning finger. And Dad said, "Quiet, let's sneak up and surprise him."

"It's almost cruel to stop Barney," Mother said. "I feel like yelling myself."

Dad softly opened the door of the car and slid out. He opened the back door for Barney and Mother got out the far side of the car. In a soft-footed row they tiptoed over to Grandpa, then they stood close so as to cast their shadows over Grandpa's busy hands. Grandpa was saying things under his breath to the messed-up line and was annoyed at the shadow. He looked up. "Barney!" he yelled. He got up and just stood.

Then Grandpa did a strange thing. He started toward Barney, turned back, and ran to the barn. He gave a hard shove and closed the barn door. Then he came back, hoisted Barney, and held him above his head. "Golly," he yelled, "what a right time for you to come home. Grandma and I were getting snowed under with that store and the blasted rabbits. Will Grandma ever welcome you! But it'll be no surprise. You know those feelings she gets? Well, from six o'clock last night she just knew you were coming. She didn't sleep all night—she wanted to be awake and feel you coming closer and closer. She kept me awake, but I didn't feel a thing but downright sleepy. You three are sure a sight for no-sleep eyes."

Grandpa wiped his no-sleep eyes. "Go and show yourselves to Grandma," he told Mother and Dad. "She went to the store early to get it in apple-pie shape, she was so sure you'd be here. If she can tend the store without one wink of sleep all night, you two ought to be able to manage it, even after driving all night. That is, if you're staying."

"We're staying," Father said.

"Oh, we're staying all right. We're back to stay, but what kind of welcome is this?" Mother said suspiciously. "Why do you need to get rid of us so fast, and what about Barney—and why can't you tend the store?"

Grandpa looked uneasy. "Well, don't you think Barney and I ought to celebrate a day like this with a bit of fishing?" he said with a small grin. Then he was serious. "No, we'll be along. It's that I've got to be alone with Barney a while. You see—oh, I hate to say this—I sold the rabbits. Came darn near renting your house, too, but the fellow backed out at the last minute. I was lucky there, but I wasn't lucky with the rabbits—so don't you think you'd better leave us alone a little while?"

"Oh, yes!" Mother sucked in her breath.

Father grabbed her hand and ran with her to the car. Then they came running back, Mother with Rosita, Dad with the goldfish bowl. Mother handed Rosita to Barney, and Grandpa stood woodenly with the goldfish bowl in his gnarled old hands. He kept looking into the bowl. "Just yesterday," he said into the bowl, "just yesterday I sold them. If only you'd come home one day sooner!" Then as the car wheeled out of the yard, Grandpa set the goldfish bowl down, put his hands on Barney's shoulders, and said again as if it were a slow, sad song, "Just yesterday I sold them, hutches and all."

"All of them?" Barney asked woefully.

"Every blasted rabbit," Grandpa said. "All thirty. All that's left is their smell."

Barney shoved Rosita toward Grandpa and flung the barn door open. Grandpa came slowly in with the goldfish and Rosita, tail up, followed him. There, there against the back wall where thirty wire hutches had risen up from the floor stood one brand-new fish pole. With the fish pole he'd been working on, Grandpa sort of tiptoed to the back wall, tiptoed as if he were in church, and set his own pole beside the pole standing there.

Barney stood there with Rosita. Then Grandpa picked up the fish bowl and set it in the great empty space where the hutches had been.

There was nothing to say, but he must say something. His own Grandpa tiptoeing! He'd never done that before!

Barney tried a little joke. "Grandpa, I had thirty rabbits and now I've got two goldfish—and a cat!"

"Two fish and a cat," Grandpa echoed. "Oh, and of course, that new fish pole is yours. But listen, with all the money from the rabbits, I bought us a boat. A white boat will match your white cat. If that's a help?"

"Oh, that's a lot," Barney said. "Grandpa, that's a lot —even a boat!" He couldn't help it that a quaver stayed in his voice.

"The rowboat's already in the river," Grandpa said.

"In that little bay where the swimming hole is. There's catfish down there in the shadows."

"No rabbits," Barney said to himself. The barn was too big for two fish poles, two goldfish and one white cat.

"No rabbits," Grandpa said as if he'd heard Barney's thoughts. "But no hutches, either, no hutches to clean every day after school and almost all day Saturday."

Barney picked Rosita up, but she wiggled free. She wanted to sniff the whole wall where the hutches had been. Her pink nose crinkled and wrinkled and snuffed, and then she sneezed. Finally she sat down to wash her whiskers clean from her sneezes.

Grandpa and Barney watched her. There was nothing to say but something had to be said: "Cats are clean," Barney told Grandpa. "You don't have to clean cats."

"Yes," Grandpa agreed. "You start out with one cat and that's often how it stays, you *have* one cat. But you start out with one rabbit and soon you have thirty rabbits, and thirty hutches to clean. And by the time you get them cleaned there's thirty more rabbits—or that's the way it seems, sometimes. You've got a barn full of rabbits and a hide full of work—work and no fishing. Work all your free day from school, and then it's time for school again."

"There's no school for me today," Barney said.

"It's Friday," Grandpa told him. "And I heard the first

bell when I was working on the fish pole, so if you don't just stand there looking at me you can still make it before the tardy bell. But it does seem a little bit foolish to start school on a Friday, doesn't it?"

Barney nodded his head.

Grandpa was figuring something. "We could take the old delivery truck," he said. "Now your Dad's here with his car—we could go fishing on your first day home—but of course there *is* school."

"There's always school," Barney said.

Grandpa grinned. "It does seem that into each life some school must fall," he said. "In fact, quite a lot. But not today."

Barney laughed, not because it was so funny but because it was strange. Dad had to tease him about school when he was happy, and Grandpa because he felt uneasy, but it meant nothing at all. And everybody knew it. Then he looked at the goldfish standing in the great bare space of the hutches, and he had an idea.

"Grandpa," he said, "Grandpa, I know what we can do so the barn won't look so empty. We'll put a big metal tank, like what cows drink from, in place of the hutches, then every time we go fishing we'll bring the small ones we catch home, and keep them in the tank until they grow big. Fish don't smell—not under water."

"Not on your life, Barney! You would think of something like that, but you won't catch me. I know you! One tank and soon there'd be a barnful of tanks. Then instead of feeding and cleaning rabbits, you'd have me combing out the wet whiskers of all the miserable catfish in the tanks. No, thank you!"

Barney laughed. Then Grandpa laughed too. And then they laughed together, and the sound filled the barn.

"If we went fishing now," Barney asked, "could Rosita come too? She won't be any trouble, she's a smart cat, she can open doors. And, Grandpa, know why I brought the goldfish? It's to set them free in our river."

Grandpa went and picked up the fish poles. Barney scooped up Rosita, squeezed her under one arm, and grabbed the goldfish bowl.

Grandpa was already climbing into the truck. He looked down at Barney, Rosita, and the goldfish. "Let's set all of us free," he said. "First we must show you and your cat to Grandma, and the new fish poles to your dad, and then let's go fishing, and the first catfish we catch— let's set him free with your goldfish."

Grandpa roared the truck, Barney climbed in, and they were on their way.

When they stopped, there was Grandma in the grocery store, Mother and Dad too, all in white working coats and all talking.

Grandma hugged him, and tiny as she was, tried to lift

him off the floor. Barney was a little embarrassed, so he quick kissed her, and showed Rosita to her.

Dad was envying him and Grandpa the new fish poles and Grandpa told Dad, "If you let us go fishing today, we'll tend store and deliver groceries for you tomorrow. You can go fishing in our new boat too, and, by golly, you can use our new poles—both of them!"

"It's a deal," Dad said. "Leave a few fish in the river for me."

They got in the truck and Barney turned around to wave goodbye, sort of choked up with all the excitement. But Grandpa poked him. Grandpa held up a comb—he'd taken a new comb from the store! "To comb out the wet whiskers of the first catfish we catch," Grandpa said. "Before you set him free with the goldfish."

In his excitement Barney could do nothing but hug Rosita, and when he felt sure Grandpa wasn't looking, he kissed her.

BOOKS BY MEINDERT DeJONG

Published by The Macmillan Company

THE ALMOST ALL-WHITE RABBITY CAT

THE EASTER CAT

A HORSE CAME RUNNING

Published by Harper & Row, Inc.

ALONG CAME A DOG

THE BIG GOOSE AND THE LITTLE WHITE DUCK

THE CAT THAT WALKED A WEEK

DIRK'S DOG BELLO

FAR OUT THE LONG CANAL

GOOD LUCK DUCK

THE HOUSE OF SIXTY FATHERS

HURRY HOME, CANDY

JOURNEY FROM PEPPERMINT STREET

THE LAST LITTLE CAT

THE LITTLE COW AND THE TURTLE

THE MIGHTY ONES

NOBODY PLAYS WITH A CABBAGE

PUPPY SUMMER

SHADRACH

THE SINGING HILL

SMOKE ABOVE THE LANE

THE TOWER BY THE SEA

THE WHEEL ON THE SCHOOL

About the Author

Meindert DeJong has won the three most distin-
guished honors a children's book author can re-
ceive: the Newbery Medal in 1955 for *The
Wheel on the School,* the Hans Christian An-
dersen International Award in 1962, and the
National Book Award for Children's Literature
in 1969 for *Journey from Peppermint Street.*

Mr. DeJong was born in Wierum, Holland,
and came to the United States when he was a
boy. He and his wife have lived in Michigan and
in Mexico, and now live in Chapel Hill, North
Carolina.